STRAW
BOSS

Center Point
Large Print

Also by E. E. Halleran and available from
Center Point Large Print:

The Far Land

STRAW BOSS

E. E. HALLERAN

CENTER POINT LARGE PRINT
THORNDIKE, MAINE

Principal Characters

YOUNG JOHNNY MORAN
His accidental breaking up of a rustlers' outfit gets him trouble.

RANCE WHITAKER
Hires Johnny as a detective on the basis of his new reputation.

BILLY
Rance's hellcat blonde daughter. She can outride and outshoot most men.

THE BUCKALEWS
A hard-bitten father and his sons, they terrorize the valley until a green cowhand stops them cold with his guns—and luck.

Chapter One

MOST of the XT boys were preparing to ride on a fence repair chore when the nighthawk brought word of the raid. Ten of old Barlow's finest brood mares had been stolen during the night. For the third time in as many weeks the mysterious horse thieves of the Raton Basin had gotten clean away with some particularly valuable stock.

The men around the corrals and the harness shop didn't wait for Old Man Barlow to come storming out. Already they had listened to his comments on the subject of horse thieves in general and of this band in particular. The comments had been violent and profane—and uncomplimentary to the trackers who had failed to run down the outlaws. Now that this bunch of blooded stock was missing every man in the outfit knew that the fiery old rancher would outdo all previous performances. Better to start moving than to be on hand when he started to cuss.

Men who had not already saddled their broncs for the day's work did so in a hurry while others rushed to pick up the gun belts they had stashed away. Regular chores at XT would not be handled today.

Johnny Moran was one of those who dashed for his gun. At least he started to do so, completely ignoring the fact that he had been holding one end of a heavy reel of barbed wire. His sudden move threw the unwieldy bulk against the cowpoke who had been helping him to load it into a wagon and there was an instant roar of indignant protest.

"Grab a-holt o' that bobwire, yo' rattle-headed polecat!"

Johnny turned back, a sheepish grin making his round face seem particularly like that of some urchin who had been caught tracking mud into a clean kitchen. With a quick lunge he caught up the reel, elevating it into the wagon while the other man swore and rubbed at hands which had been scraped by the barbs.

"Sorry, bud," Johnny said. Then he was running for the bunkhouse.

Another XT man swung in beside him as they raced for the door. Johnny was still grinning with excitement but the other man growled with open scorn, "Ease down, Stupe. Take it easy or yuh'll be tryin' to ride out without a saddle!"

A third man appeared in the doorway, buckling on a cartridge belt as he tried to pass. "Not Stupe!" he exclaimed. "That lunkhead would forget his hoss!"

"Dry up!" Johnny retorted, edging past his tormentors. He didn't enjoy the reputation he had gained at XT—and he didn't care for the nickname which the crew was calling him—but he had to admit that it was mostly his own fault. Enthusiasm tended to make him careless of details and it always seemed to turn out that the forgotten details drew attention. There was the calf-branding incident, for example. Moran had tried to warn his fellow cowpokes that an enraged mama cow was aiming to take vengeance upon the men who were treating her offspring so roughly. Unfortunately he had gestured with a hand that held a hot branding iron and the business end of the iron had jammed squarely against the seat of Whitey Olewine's levis. Whitey had never been able to appreciate the good intentions behind the accident.

Just now Moran was not too much concerned with the known fact that his fellow cow hands thought him either dumb, careless, or completely dangerous. For the moment it was enough to know that there would be no bobwire hauling for today. He grabbed his gun belt and hustled back into the open, swinging into the saddle of the jug-headed roan which he had selected for the day's work. He was a little sorry he wasn't forking the long-legged black which was his own private property but there was no time to change saddles now. Already men were stringing out along the trail which led up Arriba Creek, heading toward the spot where the missing stock had been pastured.

Ten minutes hard riding put Moran on the scene of action. Already a pair of XT men had picked up the sign and were shouting the word to the stream of new arrivals. The stolen mares had been herded toward the creek by four riders, the sign indicating that the raid had taken place shortly before dawn. That meant less than four hours' start for the thieves. Maybe this time the daring raiders would not be able to escape as cleverly as they had done on those earlier swoops.

Old Man Barlow arrived right behind Moran, his wizened face so red that it seemed he might explode. He sputtered angrily even while listening to the report of the first trackers but then he spat out orders which were smart and to the point.

"Two men on the ridge there to the south. A couple more cross the crick and make fer the high ground. The rest of us head upstream and stick to the sign. Gulden and Curtiss take the ridge. Moran and Olewine the other side o' the crick. Mebbe ye might spot the varmints sooner'n we could do it from down here. Hustle it up!"

Whitey Olewine glowered. "Gimme somebody else, boss. That Stupe is apt to shoot me outa sheer dumbness."

"Git!" Barlow snapped. "Likely he couldn't even hit ye."

There was a general chuckle as men plunged into their tasks while Moran tried to keep his grin. It was pretty irritating that the habit of baiting Johnny Moran should continue even at a time like this.

Olewine continued the treatment as they splashed through the shallows of Arriba Creek. "Got any shells in yore gun, Stupe?" he inquired.

"Cut it!" Moran retorted. "I get kinda tired o' the same old jokes all the time."

Something in his tone made the other cow-puncher's face straighten. It wasn't often that Moran took offense but on a couple of occasions he had made life mighty unhappy for men who had gone too far with their remarks. Johnny Moran might have the face of a mere youngster but his fists were full sized and the lanky body could exert an astonishing amount of speed and power. The XT boys generally managed to rawhide Johnny just as long as his grin lasted. When he stopped grinning they usually found something else to do.

"Shucks, Johnny," Whitey protested. "We ain't holdin' nothin' agin yuh." He laughed at his own humor as he added, "Not even me—and yuh shore held somethin' agin me. A hot brandin' iron."

Moran's good humor came back at once. "That was the stunt," he agreed. "One o' my dumbest. But now let's stick to business. The old man's goin' to plumb bust his corset if we don't catch up with the thieves this time."

11

They climbed rapidly to the crest of the rise which flanked the winding creek on its north side. Both of them scanned the rolling greens and tans of the grasslands ahead but there was nothing to reward the appraisal. Here and there small bunches of cattle grazed contentedly but there was no sign of riders.

"Headed fer the hills," Olewine suggested. "That's what they always do."

"We figure," Moran added.

The other man nodded soberly as they moved out to act as flankers for the trailing party along the creek. Twice before posses had started out on just such occasion as this and each time the trail had been lost by men who were supposed to be excellent sign readers. The obvious supposition was that the raiders had slipped away into the rocky fastnesses of the Packsaddles to the north or across the steeper Diablo range to the south. Beyond that any man could make his own guess for each trail had disappeared mysteriously but completely.

Twice the men on the higher ground had to halt while their companions along the creek studied the ground. On the second occasion Moran commented. "They're gettin' proddy down there. Mebbe I oughta find out what's wrong."

"Who'd tell yuh?" Olewine retorted. "Stick to the hills and I'll swing down to see what's wrong."

Moran covered nearly a quarter mile while his companion was making the move. They were working into the foothill country near the head of the creek, the main arc of the Packsaddles looming closer on the right. Olewine looked faintly troubled when he returned to his place. "Looks like we might be in fer it again," he greeted. "The sign disappeared into the crick jest after we left the boys. They been huntin' fer the spot where the thieves came out but they can't find it."

"Maybe they doubled back."

Olewine shook his head. "Now yuh're bein' stupid again. A dozen men have covered that ground downstream—and anyway the move woulda put the rustlers too close to the home ranch. It ain't likely they'd have risked it."

"But this is a long way to drive horses in the water, even if they knew how to avoid that deep pool back there."

"That's what's worryin' the boss. He's beginnin' to think they've missed the sign somewhere. There's so many tracks down there now that the readin' ain't too easy."

Almost as he spoke there was a movement on the lower level. The men who had been riding the creek bank broke out in several directions, one of them heading straight for Moran and Olewine.

"We missed the sign," he announced glumly as he came within speaking distance. "The devils are smart—but we'll try another way. Barlow says fer yuh to circle wide into the foothills. If yuh spot the sign o' fourteen hosses fire yuhr gun twice. Git goin'!"

Moran took the wide swing, heading straight toward the heart of the rugged Packsaddles before angling slightly left. It seemed reasonable to believe that the horse thieves might have employed some clever dodge for getting clear of the creek but would not find it practical to continue using the ruse for any great distance. Somewhere back here in the foothill country the trail should show up—unless the line of retreat ran toward the other range.

The thought made Moran increasingly eager. His fellow waddies had rawhided him about his blundering until some of them actually thought him stupid. Maybe this would be his opportunity to show them a thing or two. Let the others range the lower hills where the sign was probably faked; he'd drift back into the rough country and hunt for the real trail.

He realized that he was swinging too far to the west so he circled back, figuring that his best chance of success was to assume a raider trick and try for a counter-move. Even though he felt rather pleased with his own analysis of the situation he was not quite prepared for the discovery when it came. He had swung down from a sort of ledge, crossing a wash which in springtime would carry a substantial mountain creek into the Arriba. Now it was merely damp in the middle but the dampness served to show up some very clear prints. Fourteen horses! Moran grunted happily. Even for a man whose arithmetic was sometimes open to question this was enough.

He urged the roan forward, hunching lean shoulders as though to help the bronc up the opposite slope where the sign dwindled as it met drier ground. At the top of the rise he halted, letting a big, freckled hand drop to his gun butt. For an instant he had an urge to follow the trail alone, just to show the other jaspers what a good man could do, but then he elected to follow orders. It was the sensible thing to do.

His left hand went soothingly to the roan's neck as he used his right hand to draw the gun and fire two shots into the air. The horse bucked only for an instant and then Moran sat quietly, watching for some answering signal. Presently he saw Olewine come into view on a neighboring hill while almost as promptly another man appeared at a slightly greater distance. Johnny swung his hat until he had caught their attention, then he sent the roan at a good pace along the raider trail. He had passed the word but he did not intend to relinquish his leadership. This was going to be a job in which Johnny Moran could claim some distinction.

There was no particular difficulty in following

the sign. The ground here in the hills was soft enough so that even an indifferent tracker like Moran could have no great trouble. Johnny didn't try to fool himself that he was a wizard at reading sign but he wasn't blind enough to lose a clear trail like this one. Twice he heard double shots behind him but the sound only made him more anxious to keep his lead. This time the XT boys could follow "Stupe" Moran. Maybe they wouldn't be so cocky in the future.

An hour of steady riding took him into higher country along the shoulder of the first big ridge of the Packsaddle. Only once did he have trouble in sticking to the trail. At one point the outlaws had sent their stolen mares along a rocky outcropping which betrayed no sign at all but Moran did not let himself become bothered by it. The fourteen sets of tracks had disappeared upon a rocky ledge which led nowhere except back into the deeper tangles of the mountains. He simply had to follow that ledge to come upon the sign once more. Still it was a relief when everything worked out the way he had figured it.

Twice he paused to look over his back trail from convenient high points but never did he spot any of the other XT men. That suited him fine. He didn't mind leading them to the quarry but he wanted to get there first.

Now the trail led across the end of the big ridge, cutting back into a veritable wilderness where

XT men rarely ventured. It was entirely strange to Moran but he knew its general layout. Wooded gulches, rugged spurs of rock, and abrupt peaks extended for some fifty miles to the north. To the west the land sloped irregularly away into the upper Rio Grande Basin while eastward there was a similar drop toward the watersheds of both the Pecos and the Canadian. An outlaw stronghold in this country would have several advantages, the foremost being that stolen stock might be sent out in any of several directions.

"Ranchers of the Raton Basin had frequently tried to locate some such outlaw hangout but never had their efforts borne fruit. Once through Wild Horse Gulch there was only that pine-clad stretch of peaks and gulleys, a wilderness which might hide a veritable army. If there was an outlaw roost in the Packsaddles it was a well-concealed spot. Certainly no posse had ever been able to find it.

Midday came and went. Twice Moran halted to rest his bronc but each time the halt was a brief one. It didn't seem possible that the raiders could be making very fast time with their stolen stock and Johnny wanted to continue gaining upon them if possible.

The afternoon sun was beginning to dip behind some of the taller peaks when the trail disappeared abruptly. One minute it was clear and distinct on the sparsely grassed floor of the

17

gulley. Then it was gone. Not a hoofprint showed anywhere. Moran pulled up with a grunt of disgust. "Musta had wings," he muttered aloud, scratching one big ear with a long finger. "I could figure how they worked it at the creek but there's no water here to hide tracks."

For an instant he regretted that he had not waited for one of the more expert trackers to join him but then he swung out of the saddle to examine the ground more carefully. This disappearance of the sign had to mean something pretty important and there was no reason why Johnny Moran couldn't unravel the puzzle as well as the next man. He only hoped it wouldn't delay him long enough for the others to catch up.

He stamped a little, getting the circulation back into his long legs before leading the roan slowly along in the direction the sign had been leading. Logic suggested that the fading sign had to be another trick; fourteen horses don't fly away.

A scattering of green pine needles gave him the hint he needed. Loose needles didn't stay green very long and most of the ones on the ground were well browned with age. Those fresh ones hinted that someone might have used pine branches to sweep the trail, knocking off a few needles in the process.

It made Johnny feel pretty good to find such evidence and to think up an explanation for it. "Stupe" Moran, hey? Maybe he'd show them.

He paused to study the terrain around him, trying to outguess the outlaws. The heavy stand of pine which covered both sides of the gulley made it almost impossible for him to estimate the nature of the rising ground on either side but he guessed that he was in a narrow passage between two peaks or ridges. It seemed like a strange spot for the outlaws to have blotted a trail when there was no way to travel except straight ahead through the gulley.

The thought brought its own answer. There must be another outlet, a passage which was completely hidden. To keep it hidden the raiders had gone to a rather elaborate length. Suddenly Moran knew that he was on a hot scent now; maybe he was on the verge of finding the mysterious rustler hangout which the Basin's cattlemen had hunted so hopelessly.

He felt the tension come into him as he moved forward again, scanning the earth for green needles. The afternoon light was beginning to fail down here in the hollow but there was still plenty for the purpose. When a man knew what to look for it was even easy. A full fifty yards showed him nothing new but then he realized that there were no more bits of green showing. This part of the gulley floor had not been swept. He was almost trembling as he turned back. There had to be a side passage somewhere, probably up one of those slopes. The nature of the rustler ruse could not be explained in any other way.

He loosened the .45 in its holster, a bony thumb testing the hammer gently. The move reminded him of something. He had not replaced the spent cartridges after firing the signal.

"Stupe" Moran! That was the sort of thing which had brought him his unhappy reputation. He was glad no one else knew of the oversight. Halting long enough to reload he swung back along the left slope, still watching for those telltale needles. In a few spots where the ground was bare beneath the trees he could even make out the marks of the sweeping, and careful study soon disclosed the general limits of the trail blotters' activity. He could only hope that he could untangle the puzzle before any of the others arrived.

It was soon evident that the western slope was not the important one. No one had passed along it and the fringe of swept ground scarcely extended above the floor of the gulch. By the time he was sure of that fact he found himself back at his starting point. There were the tracks he had followed so far, the tracks which had ceased to exist because someone had been careful to have it so.

This time he was looking at them from short range and he suddenly saw something which gave him a heavy jolt. These were not the tracks of shod horses!

Almost frantically he cast about him in search of other sign but he knew without looking that there were no other tracks. These were the marks he had been following for some six or seven hours. No wonder the other XT boys hadn't caught up with him. They had spotted the nature of the trail at first sight and had refused to be fooled into trailing one of the wild horse herds which were known to roam the Packsaddles. Moran almost blushed at the thought of what they must be saying about him back there in the foothills.

Then his confusion faded as abruptly as it had come. Wild horses hadn't blotted a trail! Maybe this was the answer to a lot of things. Maybe . . .

He thought back hurriedly but with grim care. There had been no slip along the way, even at the rock ledge. This was the same sign he had picked up in that draw. He couldn't be certain but it seemed to him that he could even remember what the sign looked like back there. Unshod hoofs. Somehow the thieves had managed to pull the shoes from both stolen stock and their own mounts, counting on having their trail mistaken for wild horse sign. Probably that had been their scheme on those earlier raids. It accounted for the mysterious disappearance of their trail. Certainly it had fooled everyone—and would have fooled them again if Johnny Moran hadn't been just dumb enough to be smart.

He was grinning ruefully at himself as he picked up the search once more. That was why they had fired those signals behind him. They had been trying to call him away from what they thought was a false trail.

It brought a sobering realization. Probably no one was coming along to back him. He was getting close to the outlaw hideout but he was alone. Maybe it didn't pay to be so smart with dumbness.

Still he went forward, skirting what seemed to be the edge of the blotted area along the eastern slope. This time he found the trail quite promptly. Three recently cut pine branches lay there, evidently discarded as the trail blotters completed their chore. The marks of bootheels showed prominently beyond them and Moran could see where the men had remounted to close in on the trail of the stolen horses. Every mark was that of an unshod bronc but it didn't matter now; wild horses didn't leave marks of bootheels and they didn't sweep away their tracks with pine branches.

He was a bit jittery with excitement as he climbed back into the saddle. This was working out pretty well after all. With a little luck he might be able to locate the rustler roost and return to lead a real force to clean it out. It would certainly be a triumph for a man who was even now being discussed as a foolish blunderer.

The roan took the slope easily in spite of fatigue, Moran watching the clear sign as he considered his next moves. Five minutes later he found himself on a narrow bench which cut the northern shoulder of a ridge. From below, the bench was not noticeable but from its outer rim Moran could see most of the rough country he had recently traversed. Ahead he could see that the trail led toward an unsuspected break in the chain of peaks. Without question this was the answer to the whole outlaw problem. Rustlers and horse thieves had found themselves a hideout which made them quite safe from the efforts of vengeful ranchers.

The sun was brightening only the tops of the mountains by that time and Moran knew that he would have to work fast to learn more before night. The sign was plain enough now and he rode forward at a good pace, only slowing when the trail led between overhanging rock walls. This notch was the real entrance to the outlaw stronghold, he believed. It was here that he would have to be on watch for some kind of picket. Even though they might feel sure of their hidden retreat it seemed likely that they would post a guard.

He bent over to study the sign a little more closely but lost all interest in it as a slug whined just overhead. With the vicious sound came the crack of a rifle and Moran fairly threw himself from the saddle, taking cover under the rocky overhang and pulling the roan to safety. There had been just a split second for him to see the heavy brows and close-set eyes of a rifleman up there on the rimrock, a rifleman who was staring angrily over the sights of a Winchester. The man was not fifty feet away and Moran realized that his own movement had saved him a bullet in the head. For the moment sheer luck had saved him but the fat was in the fire. That sniper would not miss again, not at such short range, and other outlaws would soon rally to the defense of their citadel. Johnny Moran was going to have his hands full to make any use of the things he had learned. In fact, Johnny Moran was going to have his hands full to keep himself alive.

Chapter Two

THERE was a brief interval of flat silence as Moran caught his breath and listened for the outlaw sentry's next move. When nothing happened he dropped the reins over the bronc's head and edged out a little, trying to spot the rifleman. Somewhat to his surprise he was just in time to see the man disappearing at a dead run. Apparently the sentinel was more concerned about spreading the alarm than he was about killing the interloper . . . probably because he did not suspect that the intruder was so completely alone.

Moran went after him promptly, figuring that he might gain something by putting on a show of boldness. The move brought him out of the rocky little defile and into a deep cup-shaped valley which nestled high among the peaks. It was a beautiful spot but for the moment Moran was in no mood to admire the scenic beauties of the valley; all he could afford to look at was the man who had run out into the open ahead of him. Already the fellow was shouting the alarm.

Another voice shouted a hoarse reply while a rifle slapped a staccato answer from the nearest woodland. Moran knew that once more a bullet had narrowly missed his head. He drove for the shelter of a rocky outcropping, realizing that at least one other member of the outlaw gang had spotted him. At the same time the running sentry turned and dropped to one knee, slamming in a couple of hasty shots as Moran flung himself into the shelter of the rock.

Johnny could hear the slugs whining off into space as they glanced from the sheltering spike of sandstone and it seemed to him that there was an angry frustration in their whine. It was a fair warning. This outlaw band would not relax until they had gotten rid of the man who had stumbled across their hideout. Already a number of distant voices were taking up the alarm, shouting it on to men who must be at the far side of the valley.

"Looks like I got 'em, all right," Moran told himself with a wry grin. "Now what am I goin' to do with 'em? Wish I had somethin' bigger than a six-gun."

His bit of cover wasn't very large but he made its smallness work for him. He stretched out flat behind the rock, having placed his battered Stetson on the ground at his feet, and gradually nudged it away with one toe until its appearance drew enemy fire. Then he stuck his head out from the opposite side of the rock and banged away at the still kneeling rifleman. It was snap shooting under difficulties but he knew the satisfaction of making his man jump. A quick look of alarm came across that dark, narrow face and the outlaw retreated hastily into the nearest brush.

Then a bullet from a slightly different angle smashed into the ground almost at Moran's elbow and he pulled back out of sight, uneasily aware that his haste had put him into a mighty hot spot. His sign reading told him that there were at least four men ahead and he could guess that there would be several other gunmen in the hangout. One man with a six-gun didn't have much chance against that kind of odds.

In the lull after the little skirmish he heard two distant gunshots and felt a little better. Some XT rider must have heard the shooting in the high country. Now maybe Barlow's boys would realize that "Stupe" Moran hadn't been chasing any shadows—or wild horses.

Still Moran realized that those signal shots were mighty far away. For the moment he had the protection of a little knob of rock but it wouldn't take long for his enemies to work around the rim of the valley and flank his position. Then they would have him at the mercy of a deadly cross-fire.

It wasn't a pretty prospect. At least two competent riflemen were keeping him pinned in his present dangerous spot. Only reinforcements or darkness could help him and he didn't feel optimistic about either. There would be enough light for shooting for at least an hour, in which interval he didn't believe help could arrive.

"Trust me!" he muttered aloud. "Nobody but Johnny Moran could bust into a mess like this. Sometimes I wonder what I've got between the ears."

He tried the hat trick again, shoving the Stetson into view on the end of his gun barrel. This time he almost lost the gun as a well-directed slug drilled the hat and ticked the gun muzzle. That was enough for Moran. He was really pinned down—by a marksman who could put a bullet exactly where he wanted it.

That fact established, Moran took time out to study the ground around him. Directly in his rear was the opening of the ravine through which he had entered the valley. On both sides of it the ground rose steeply to form the valley walls but at a little distance the slopes became somewhat more gradual, carrying their burden of pines in neat waves up and out of the valley proper. Obviously that slope would be the real danger spot. The outlaws could send riflemen through the trees to take position on that elevated ground. Then Moran would be a dead duck.

"Only one thing to do," he told himself grimly. "I can't wait around to be the kind of a target they want."

He gathered his long legs under him, tensing for his break even as he listened for sounds which might give him a hint as to the location of his more dangerous foes. Then he showed himself for a split second on the left side of the rock, whirling back out of sight to dash full-tilt into the open at the opposite side. The diversion permitted him to gain a good five yards before guns could shift to cover him. At the first shot he cut sharply, breaking for the trees in his rear. Two weapons were firing now but the maneuver seemed to have upset both marksmen. Three or four slugs whined past him harmlessly and he risked one turn to drive a couple of bullets into the trees where the smoke was beginning to rise. It was then that he felt his left arm go numb.

He made a frantic dive for cover, lying there breathless while those angry hornets smashed through the foliage above his head. He wanted to learn what had happened to his arm but he didn't care to risk sitting up while those bullets were hunting him so stubbornly. Then the firing ceased and he could hear shouts again. The outlaw leader was changing his orders, calling off the flankers who had started up the slopes. In another minute the whole pack would be closing in for a mass attack.

It was then that the pain began to make itself felt in the numbed arm and he saw that the back of the arm had been raked nastily by a slug. The bullet must have come from directly behind him, catching the arm as it swung while he was running. It was only a flesh wound, he thought, but it was bleeding badly and needed attention.

He ripped clumsily at the sleeve, finally using his knife to cut a strip of cloth with which to bind the arm as best he could. Then he crawled hastily back into deeper cover, trying to find a spot where he could set up his defense.

There was little time for the maneuver. Already he could hear men working through the brush toward him and before he could set himself properly he spotted a burly rifleman coming through the trees. The rustler saw him almost at the same moment and two weapons swung simultaneously. At this range, however, the easier-handled Colt had the advantage and Moran blasted grimly, uneasily aware that he had not reloaded his gun since the fight opened.

His second shot sent the enemy sprawling and Moran edged back again, fumbling to reload while holding the gun in the still partly paralyzed left hand. It was painful work but he forced himself to it, knowing that he could expect no quarter from the outlaws whose secret he had discovered. This time he loaded all six chambers, scorning the usual safety measure of leaving an empty under the hammer. A man had no use for empty chambers at a time like this.

He had a brief respite then, using the time to work at the bandage on his arm. Another slash at his shirt provided him with a pad and he tied the wad into place, trying to stop the flow of blood. A slug smashed into a tree beside him just as he was completing the effort and he rolled to draw a fine bead on a skulking figure to his right. Again there was a brisk exchange of fire and once more he knew that he had been downright lucky. There was no time for self-congratulation over the good shooting, however; already the darkening wood-land seemed full of stealthy sounds. Men were advancing upon him from several angles and he could only try for a better position, hopeful of avoiding a concentrated charge.

After that he lost count of both time and events. Gunfire seemed to be all around him and he traded shots with someone every time he moved. Reloading was becoming difficult, not only because of the bad arm but because the enemy was not giving him a breathing spell. It was just a case of fire, duck away, then fire again. The arm was aching painfully and he knew that another bullet had creased his thigh but there was no time to examine the new injury. He had a feeling that he must have fired at some fifteen or twenty different enemies but even in the whirl of dim impressions he knew he was exaggerating. Not that it mattered. He had to keep fighting, hope-ful that either darkness or reinforcements would arrive.

Darkness seemed the more likely bet. Already the battle had dragged on for many minutes and the woodland was becoming heavy with evening shadows. A little more delay . . .

Then two men drove at him savagely, firing as they came. He cut them down with the same grim precision that had accounted for his first enemy but he knew that he had been struck again. Pain went through him in waves until he was not certain where the wound was located. He struggled to keep his eyes open, only half aware that silence had settled upon the immediate vicinity. It didn't give him any particular consolation. There was only the dreary knowledge that he was losing his grip. The world was getting darker than those night shadows warranted. He tried to gather himself for another evasive movement but the effort was too much for his faltering senses. The blackness simply deepened until he knew no more.

The sun was high above pine-clad peaks when Moran opened his eyes to the realization that he was miraculously alive. For some minutes he was content to lie quiet, the brief motions of awakening having started pains all over his body. Memory gradually flooded back and he tried to recall those final dim moments of the fight. Then clearer consciousness came and he knew that the gory details were unimportant. His present situation was all that counted. Evidently he had been unconscious throughout the night and part of the ensuing day. But where was he and what had happened? Why had the horse thief gang permitted him to live?

His answer came more quickly than he had anticipated. It was a pleasant answer even though it came in the acid tones of Old Man Barlow. "Goin' to wake up, are ye, ye dam' idjit?"

The familiar wizened form swam hazily into Johnny's range of vision, the XT boss grinning sourly through the mist. Johnny shook his head, trying to clear his eyes, but subsided abruptly as the movement brought fresh aches. "I ain't so sure," he muttered. "Somehow it don't seem worth the effort."

Barlow uttered his dry chuckle again, stooping over Moran to study him with eyes that held a twinkle. "Of all the damfool stunts!" he growled. "Why in hell didn't ye wait till some o' the rest of us could find out what ye was up to? Ain't ye got no more sense than to tackle a gang o' hoss thieves single-handed?"

"I'm not supposed to have sense," Johnny retorted. "Remember? Anyway, you got here in time."

"Only to clean up. We found four dead men and a wounded jigger. The rest of 'em got away in the dark. Looks like they went in a hurry, seein' as how they didn't finish ye off nor pick up their pard. Lucky one of our boys fell over yer carcass; ye mighta bled to death."

"How bad am I hurt?"

"Nothin' serious. Hole in yer laig, a crease across yer head, and a nick over the top o' yer shoulder. I ain't listin' the wound in yer arm because ye had that plugged up and don't need to be told about it."

"Is that all? Feels like I got more leaks in my carcass than that."

"They leaked plenty," Barlow told him soberly. "Stay quiet now. Purty soon we'll fix up a litter and haul ye down the mountain. Meanwhile there's some soup a-comin'. Better try to stomach a bit of it."

"Did you get the mares back?"

"We shore did! Likewise we picked up quite a bit of other stock. This here hideout musta been a reg'lar rustler and hoss thief bazaar!"

It was not until the following morning that they left the outlaw valley, Moran riding uncomfortably on a makeshift litter. In the interval he had slept most of the time but in his waking moments he managed to hear some of the talk around him. It seemed that the hidden valley must have been the headquarters for a small but active gang. There were two corrals and a cabin back in the woodland, a wealth of sign hinting that four men had been using the place for some days. With the four who had actually stolen the mares, that meant a total of eight in the gang Moran had fought.

Most of them had pressed home the attack on

Johnny while the others had tried to run some of the stolen stock out. Every indication showed that the herders had been called back when Moran began to fight such a deadly battle, the result being that only a few animals were taken away with the three surviving outlaws. Since Barlow's men had met no opposition it seemed safe to assume that such retreat had begun with the darkness.

The rest of the picture was not so clear. No one knew where the surviving gunmen had gone and no one had found the trail over which the stolen stock must have been customarily handled. XT men searched the immediate country but found nothing. There was another outlet on the far side of the valley but it led into a wilderness of rocky canyons which made tracking all but impossible. A future search of that badland country might reveal something but for the present there was neither time nor the supplies to make such a search.

The best prospect seemed to be that the wounded prisoner would talk. At least that had been the argument when the old man sent him down the mountain under guard, overruling the general proposal to hang him immediately. Barlow was confident that the gang was shattered, even though there was much evidence to indicate that it might have operated on a larger scale than they had guessed.

In return for this information Moran had to answer an embarrassing question. Everyone wanted to know why he had followed a trail which appeared to be that of a wild horse band. They already knew, from questioning the prisoner, that the outlaw ruse had been a carefully calculated one: risking delay to remove all shoes from the stolen stock as well as from their own horses. Then, when all sign of the work had been carefully blotted out, they could make their escape with the presumption that their trail would be ignored. At least four XT men had noted the tracks but had failed to see anything significant in them. Only Moran had elected to follow the trail and the other men wanted to know why.

Johnny decided that he wasn't going to expose himself to any further humor. For once he was in a good position and he intended to stay there. Pretending a weakness which was all too close to being real he merely waved the question aside. "Shucks," he said. "Anybody with half an eye could spot the difference between wild horse prints and the kind o' trail them hombres made. Wild horses don't stay bunched so regular—and they don't keep goin' on such a straight line." Then he added as a clincher, "And they don't stop to blot their own trails."

After that he refused to answer any questions and by the time he had taken the jolts of an hour's riding he was in no position to answer any. He didn't even know when he was lifted from the horse and carried into a room at the home ranch.

Chapter Three

TWO WEEKS PASSED before Moran could work up much interest in his surroundings. Vaguely he knew that the trip down to XT had opened a wound, leaving him both weak and feverish. Doc Glenn, the elderly medico from Sawmill Springs, had spent a lot of time with him but there had been other visitors as well. Sheriff Lloyd had been at the ranch several times, as had Al Kincaid, editor of the Sawmill Springs *Gazette*. Even during the worst of the period Moran had realized that he was being hailed as something of a hero. He could only hope that he wouldn't get delirious and say something to spoil it.

Finally Doc Glenn let him get out of bed and he was able to hobble out to the broad porch of the ranch house, feeling weak but otherwise reasonably well mended. The move seemed to be a signal for the end of whatever orders of silence Glenn had issued. At any rate Old Man Barlow promptly brought him a copy of the *Gazette*.

"Better read this," the old man advised sourly. "If'n it don't make ye sick to yer stummick ye're a safe bet to git well again."

Johnny took the paper and read. Al Kincaid had

really spread himself in writing of the biggest bit of news to hit the country in a couple of decades. One half of the front page was devoted to a history of past outlaw raids while the other half carried a lurid account of the one-man battle which had been fought by Johnny Moran. It was told in a fine running style and Moran enjoyed it from the very first paragraph.

"Johnny Moran," it recounted, "an XT rider with the hastily gathered posse, was the man who picked up the outlaw trail. He signaled to a companion and the word was passed. When other men gathered at the point indicated by Moran, however, there was a disposition to doubt his judgment. The trail they found was that of unshod horses and the trailers believed that Moran had mistaken a wild horse trail for that of the horse thieves. Fortunately for all concerned two men were sent to overtake Moran while the rest of the posse continued the search in that part of the mountains. Consequently they were still within hearing distance when Moran began his fight.

"He had done a remarkable piece of tracking to follow the raiders to a well-concealed hideout deep in the Packsaddles but he was not satisfied to succeed where other men had failed. With great courage he attacked the outlaws single-handed, putting up an unbelievable battle until help arrived."

There was more of it, some accurate and some purely imaginative but in every detail it lauded the brains, skill and bravery of Johnny Moran. Editor Al Kincaid had really poured it on, evidently having decided that a hero story made good reading. Johnny Moran agreed with him. He liked it.

There was a grunt as Johnny looked up from one of the more imaginative paragraphs. Old Man Barlow was grinning sourly at him, evidently watching the expressions of the reader. "Plumb nauseatin', ain't it? Or do ye like bein' hailed as the bright-eyed young hero?"

Moran grinned in return. "A man can always appreciate havin' his true worth recognized," he said with great dignity. " 'Specially when he's been gettin' shoved around by dumb polecats who don't understand him."

Barlow swore disgustedly. "Ye talk like that damfool of a Kincaid. I still got a sneakin' suspicion that ye was too dumb to notice what kind o' tracks ye was followin'."

"You're just jealous," Moran told him, keeping his face straight. "How about this part on the way the thieves worked the un-shoeing business? Is that the way it happened?"

"Seems so. Leastways that's the way the prisoner told it. The crooks never stole big bunches o' stock. They picked out the best and took the time to rip off shoes. That way they figured we'd pass up their tracks—jest like we always did."

"Kinda stupid," Moran commented. "It didn't fool me."

Old Man Barlow swore again and stamped away toward the corral. Johnny chuckled at the sight of the boss's disgust, wrinkling his snub nose as he considered the way his luck had turned. "Seems like I'm quite a character," he muttered to himself. "A smart hombre and a brave hero. I reckon I'll ask for a raise."

For a full week he played it that way, taking a full measure of revenge on his annoyed fellow cowpunchers and driving Old Man Barlow into extended exhibitions of profanity.

"I ain't fooled none by all that hawgwash Kincaid put in his stinkin' old paper," Barlow raged. "Ye blundered on to that trail and was too thick-headed to notice whether it was wild hoss tracks or whatever. Then ye was stupid enough to stick yer snub nose into a hornet's nest when any sane man woulda gone fer help. Mebbe ye even kept us from ketchin' the whole kit and caboodle o' them outlaws. Ye're no hero, dammit, ye're a dag-nabbed idjit!"

Johnny merely waved his copy of the Sawmill Springs *Gazette*. "That ain't what it says here," he said quietly.

He even managed to build up the story a little so that the next edition of the paper carried a

40

revised version he had personally given to the eager Al Kincaid. Again it was a fine mixture of fact and imagination. The part about following the trail along the rock ledge and the trouble in spotting the turnoff where the horse thieves had blotted trail was good enough to stand on its own. Otherwise Johnny drew largely on his imagination. Having plenty of time to work out convincing details he built the yarn up into something which he hoped would impress the XT men and the result was another fine splurge in the *Gazette*.

By the time it appeared, Moran was almost ready for duty once more. At least he was sufficiently recovered so that he could strut among his former tormentors. In self-defense most of them had adopted Barlow's trick of claiming that the whole show had been a matter of dumb luck but Johnny showed fine scorn for such comments. He was riding high now and he intended to use the spurs while he had the opportunity.

Then came a development which slowed him up a little. Al Kincaid rode up to the XT ranch house shortly before noon one day, talking excitedly to Old Man Barlow before coming on to where Moran sat in the doorway of the harness shop mending his gun belt. Barlow came with him, an expression of disgusted surprise on his weather-beaten features.

Kincaid was clearly excited, his normally pallid

features flushed as he stuttered, "Got a wire f-f-for you, J-J-Johnny. Here." He fairly shoved it into Moran's hand. "Got it this m-m-mornin'."

Moran took it and saw that it was rather lengthy for a telegram. Sent from Dragoon Bend, it was addressed to The Editor, Sawmill Springs *Gazette*. It read:

> "AUTHORIZE YOU HIRE MORAN FOR RUSTLER CASE HERE. READY TO PAY HIS FIGURE. SITUATION OUTLINED IN YOUR PAPER THREE WEEKS AGO. NOW WORSE. GET HIM. NOTIFY ME DRAGOON BEND WHEN HE WILL ARRIVE."

It was signed simply "Whitaker."

Johnny looked up with a frown. "What does it mean?" he asked. "And who is this Whitaker?"

Kincaid answered the two questions in reverse order. "Rance Whitaker owns the Lazy J outfit over in Antelope Valley. The Antelope Valley spreads have been having more rustler trouble and they want to hire a man who has had some luck at the chore." He had stopped stuttering now.

"Luck is right!" Barlow growled.

Kincaid ignored him and pulled a newspaper from his pocket. "Here's the old issue the wire mentions. We ran a story about the way rustlers and horse thieves have been be-deviling the country. Whitaker's outfit is mentioned. Over on their side of the Packsaddles it seems to have been mostly cattle rustling while it's been horses over here—but we had an idea the same gang was handling both."

"Now it looks like mebbe ye was right," Barlow cut in, dropping his air of acid sarcasm. "That hideout in the mountains coulda been used by sech a gang. From there they could work their stolen stock down through the rough country into the upper Rio Grande Valley or they could drive it east and southeast to any one of half a dozen shippin' points on the Santa Fe."

"You think I should hire on with this Whitaker?" Moran asked.

Barlow wrinkled his nose disgustedly. "Shore. The dumb galoot deserves it—if he ain't got no better sense than to make an offer like that. Go ahead."

Kincaid looked troubled at the way Barlow was expressing it, but the grin on Moran's broad features seemed to reassure him. Apparently this was the way Old Man Barlow talked to his best men. "Shall I wire him?" he asked quickly.

"No hurry," Barlow answered before Johnny could speak up. "The crazy varmint won't be ready to ride fer a week yet. Write him a letter and tell him Moran will be there a week from next Wednesday. I'll try to put up with him that long . . . and tell Whitaker that the price is fifty dollars a week and expenses."

"Hey!" Johnny protested. "That's rubbin' it in. A ranch foreman don't draw wages like that."

"Shut up!" Barlow snapped. "Ranch foremen ain't heroes neither. Git what ye can while it's comin'. In a week Whitaker will have a bellyful of ye and ye'll be outa luck. When ye git fired I want ye to have enough dinero so we won't have ye comin' back here."

Editor Kincaid again seemed concerned about the abusive language being aimed at his pet hero. "Maybe Moran should come to Sawmill Springs right now," he suggested stiffly. "He can remain there until time to take a train to Dragoon Bend."

Old Man Barlow turned to wag a skinny finger in the newspaperman's face. "He's stayin' right here till he's got a whole hide again. I figure I owe him a bit for the job he's already done so I'll keep the ornery cuss in luxurious idleness while I try to beat a grain o' sense into his thick haid. I figger to tell him a few things about that Packsaddle country—and I'm figurin' he oughta ride through it when he heads fer Lazy J. A man don't git the feel of a country when he rides them daggone trains."

Kincaid smiled with quick relief. "That's all right," he agreed. "Does it stand with you, Moran?"

44

"Suits me. Just tell him I'll show up Wednesday week."

It was just a week later that Johnny Moran rode away from XT, speeded on his journey by a variety of comments which ranged from the sourly humorous to the skeptically worried. XT was wishing him luck but there was little confidence in his prospects of matching the accomplishments of his last bit of activity.

In the interval Old Man Barlow had been helpful without ever relaxing his severity. He brought out a map of the entire region, insisting that Moran make a detailed copy of it. "Git the country in mind, keep yer eyes open, and don't git careless. Luck won't stand by ye all the time."

He took pains to point out the manner in which the almost unexplored badlands sprawled out to form a barrier between Antelope Valley and the Raton country. There were ranches in both regions, the Packsaddles looming ominously over each.

"I'm figgerin' Whitaker's headache is the same as ours," Barlow growled. "We got to bust up one gang to clear both bits o' country. Mebbe ye're the feller to do it. Ye've got guts enough but I'm hopin' ye don't go back to bein' as dumb as ye've always been. Use yer eyes when ye ride through the badlands. It might be that ye'll pick up some ideas. Too bad that outlaw had to die before we could git him to talkin'; now ye'll have to work from scratch."

He grinned a little less sourly as he added, "Ye might as well play old Whitaker right. I know him kinda well. He's plumb educated—and lazy. All his ambition's in his wife's name and he's henpecked without knowin' it. Act plenty cocky and he'll think ye're all that Kincaid says ye are."

Moran recalled the advice as he headed into the foothills. The ride to Lazy J ought to give him a few ideas about the supposed outlaw country before he reported in for his new job. Probably he would need them.

He camped for the night in the outlaw shack at the hidden valley, content to have made that much progress. There were still a few aches from the wounds but for the most part he felt fit and ready. Which was another advantage of making the trip this way; it gave him a chance to get saddle-hardened again. And it permitted him to take the prized black pony with him.

The following day took him through the rugged country which was the real heart of the Pack-saddles. Mostly the country was cut by rocky gulches which seemed to work out in every direction and he knew why the XT men had not been able to track fleeing outlaws here. For the most part the sign would be almost impossible to follow unless a well-organized party went to work with a great amount of patience. Possible passages went in so many directions that it was purely guesswork to think that stolen stock might have moved toward any given point. Studying the map he had brought with him, he decided that there were three main possibilities. The stock might go out to the west into the upper Rio Grande Valley for shipment to the north. Or it might be shoved toward the southeast to reach the rail line near Sawmill Springs. Or a similar move might take it out through the eastern end of Antelope Valley for shipment in the neighborhood of Dragoon Bend. Since the latter two alternatives involved a certain amount of boldness on the part of the thieves it seemed natural to guess that the first one would be correct.

When the day was over he knew that he was still guessing. He had not come upon any sign that seemed at all recent and the whole journey had become pretty confusing. During the afternoon he had consulted the sun with increasing frequency to make certain that he was not getting lost in the tangle of canyons. If rustlers knew this country well enough to use it they were pretty smart.

That night he camped on the northeast slope of what he believed to be the big ridge which flanked Antelope Valley. Tomorrow—Wednesday morning—he would climb the ridge and have a look at the troubled valley before reporting. It was the sort of campaign Old Man Barlow had practically ordered but Moran could not see that it had been very successful. He hadn't seen any sign of outlaws.

Daylight showed him the notch which was supposed to offer the best passage across into the valley. He had to work his way along through more of the broken country in order to reach something which appeared like a decent approach to the climb but the time was not wasted. Less than a mile southeast of the spot where he had spent the night he found a definite trail leading into the notch. The passage had not been used recently and the sign was not at all clear but after several minutes of careful study he came to the conclusion that both horses and cattle had passed through here. There was nothing to indicate that it had ever been used for large drives but that was not surprising. One feature of the Packsaddle outlaw crowd had been their preference for stealing small bunches of especially valuable stock. What really counted here was that Moran could find no trace of either cattle or riders heading north. Every readable sign was that of hoofs going across into Antelope Valley.

It gave him something to think about as he sent the big black into the winding gulch which provided a fairly easy ascent of the big ridge. Directly across this hogback should be the valley which had been bothered so much by rustlers— but all the sign pointed in the wrong direction.

Stock had been moved across into Antelope Valley, not out of it.

He worked upward for the better part of an hour, occasionally finding ground where he could see those significant tracks again. It seemed certain that no one had come through here for at least a couple of weeks. Then it had been several riders or led horses, all going southward toward Antelope Valley. He counted back over the time he had been laid up with his wound, wondering whether this could be the trail of the survivors of the horse thief gang. The time seemed a little long but there was always the chance that good weather had preserved the tracks unusually well.

The ground seemed to be leveling out ahead of him when suddenly he caught sight of a fresh footprint in the trail. A bootheel had marked the turf quite clearly. Moran pulled up at once, studying the ground around him. At first he could not see even another single print but a dozen feet further up the trail he found what he was searching for. It seemed certain that someone had walked down the trail a short distance and had returned, still afoot. The pedestrian had kept to the edge of the brush and it seemed likely that the idea had been to keep his tracks concealed.

Johnny dismounted and studied the marks with some care. It took him quite a few minutes but eventually he was able to trace the path of the mysterious person who had chosen the ridge top for taking a stroll. The unknown one had come down the path some fifty feet and had returned the way he had come. At first there seemed to be no explanation for the move but then Moran noticed something at the point where the stranger had turned. A thick grapevine had been severed at its base, the cut clean enough to hint at a good sharp knife. Johnny studied the trees carefully and presently discovered a loose end of vine dangling from a big locust tree. Someone must have gone to the trouble of climbing the tree to make the second cut, thus securing a piece of grapevine which would be from twenty to thirty feet long. For the life of him Johnny couldn't think why anyone should want a piece of wild grapevine.

He wanted to shrug it off and go forward with his journey but Old Man Barlow's warning rang in his ears. On this job he couldn't afford to neglect anything. There wouldn't be any room for mistakes.

Picketing the black bronc at the side of the trail he moved forward afoot, studying the trail of the man who had come down the slope for the vine. Within a dozen paces he found a place in the brush where some tag alders had been cut off with the same kind of efficient slash as had severed the grapevine. Here the ground sign was even fresher and Johnny decided that the mysterious cutter of vines and bushes had done his work on the previous evening.

Engrossed in his study of the ground he had not paid much attention to the trail ahead but suddenly he realized that the passage narrowed sharply. There was still about the same amount of clearance through the trees but at this one point the brush seemed to have grown out into the cleared trail. Which was a bit odd. That kind of bush wouldn't grow up in three weeks and it was almost certain that there had been quite a lot of traffic through here just a little before that.

He studied the scene suspiciously and was at once aware of a further note of discord. A wild grapevine crossed the path, apparently from a pine tree on the left to a point on the ground just to the right of the brush. That brought the suspicion to a head. That vine hadn't grown there in three weeks!

This time he ducked into the timber, studying the surrounding country with some care before circling back to the obstacle. The whole thing seemed pretty silly but he had made up his mind to be careful about everything. No more "Stupe" Moran. It wouldn't be healthy.

When it seemed certain that there were no watchers posted in the surrounding woodland he advanced toward the encroaching brush, promptly discovering that it was indeed a blind. Those low bushes had been stuck into the ground—so recently that their leaves had not begun to wilt. But what had been the object? They formed no real obstacle either to man or horse. For that matter neither did the vine; it would be a small matter to cut it away.

He was about to do the cutting when he remembered his resolution. Slashing the vine wouldn't tell him anything. He wanted to know why it was there. Accordingly he skirted the edge of the false bushes, studying the set-up with due care. It did not take long to discover that one end of the vine had been looped over a pine bough and tied securely on the far side of the tree.

Then he cut back, still keeping away from the elaborate blind. On the far side of the trail he traced the vine down into a thicker clump of brush where it obviously ended. This ought to provide some kind of an answer, he thought, so he parted the bushes carefully, staring down at the craziest contrivance he had ever seen. Lying flat on the ground was what appeared to be the stock of an old musket, hammer up and cocked. A thong of buckskin was fastened to the trigger and was held barely snug by the tension of the grapevine. Anyone tampering with the vine would discharge the gun.

"That's a fool stunt!" Moran said aloud. "The danged gun ain't even pointed toward the trail. Somebody around here must be plumb loco."

Chapter Four

IN HIS scorn for the stupid appearance of the man-trap Johnny almost made a fatal mistake. He was about to reach for the rawhide; careless of results so long as the gun was pointed in a harmless direction. His move, however, permitted him to see something which the bushes had previously concealed. There was no barrel worth mentioning on the musket. Directly in front of the lock the barrel had been sawed off—but a half dozen sticks of dynamite had been lashed fast to the open end. The old weapon was simply a clumsy but deadly contrivance for detonating enough dynamite to kill anyone within several yards. Certainly it would have been fatal for the person who moved that swinging vine.

Moran stepped back, waiting until he was sure that his fingers had regained their steadiness. Then he crossed to the pine tree where the vine was anchored, cutting carefully until the crude trip-line fell free. After that he returned to the trap and pulled in the vine until all tension was removed from the rawhide. Only then did he venture to lift the deadly device and remove the percussion cap from the nipple.

He felt a little easier when that much was

accomplished but he didn't quite breathe normally until the dynamite was removed from the sawed-off gun. By that time he knew that he held in his hands the remnants of an old Springfield musket, its six inches of barrel crammed full of powder. In itself it was a dangerous enough booby-trap but in conjunction with the dynamite it would have been viciously destructive. Someone had tried mighty hard to commit a very messy murder.

He buried the dynamite some distance back from the trail but carried the gun with him when he went back to his horse. Dynamite probably wouldn't be traceable but there was always the possibility that he might get a line on this old musket. It would be evidence and he knew that he was going to need something of the sort before long. An outlaw crowd which set man-traps would be a tough nut to crack and he would need every possible weapon against them.

He lashed the mutilated musket to his bedroll, mounting a little uneasily as he considered the probable perils of the trail ahead. It wouldn't do to assume that the dynamite trap would be the only effort on the part of the outlaws. From now on he would need every sense alert against an ambush.

Only for an instant had he doubted that he was the target of the man-trap. It seemed clear that this trail was not used by near-by ranchers and the timing of it all was pretty suggestive.

Somehow the rustlers had learned that Moran was arriving by way of the Packsaddle badlands and they had set the trap for him. There was always the possibility that some other victim had been intended but Johnny Moran told himself that he was going to figure it the other way until he learned different.

He kept his right hand close to the butt of his .45 as he went on up the grade and into the level stretch of the pass. Fragments of woods lore which he had heard but scarcely heeded in the past came to his mind and he found himself listening to the bird songs. While the birds chirped ahead of him he might feel reasonably certain that no ambusher awaited. Mostly, though, he scanned the pine forest, searching for some sign of movement or for some new arrangement of brush which might betray an ambush.

It was pretty nerve-racking business, particularly when he thought of that dynamite—which he did every time he relaxed the least bit. He knew that he had begun to work downhill again but he was well into the real slope when he noticed that the faint trail showed no prints at all. Back there on the climb there had been plenty of old sign but here there was none. Obviously there must have been some sort of hidden fork in the trail, a junction which he had missed in his anxiety over some new attack. For a moment he thought of retracing his steps but second thought deterred him. The object in riding across through the badlands had been attained—somewhat more dramatically than he had expected. Now he ought to get on with the business of reporting to Rance Whitaker.

Ten minutes later he broke out into an open patch where the pines fell away to give a clear view of the broad valley ahead. The sun was now almost at its meridian, brightening the valley so that every detail appeared sharp and clear as he studied it. Only a slight haze fuzzed the distant peaks of the Antelopes while the nearer hills and the valley's grasslands seemed to be almost within shouting distance. Moran knew that there was a good twelve miles of pasturage between the Packsaddles and the Antelopes but now it seemed only yards across.

He pulled out his map once more, checking landmarks until he was certain that he had indeed used the notch suggested by Barlow. Everything was there just as the map pictured it. Directly in front of him was a final sharp pitch to the valley itself. Some three miles of excellent grass were bordered by a line of low hills which seemed to split the long valley while over beyond the hills he could see more pasturage and a cluster of buildings which would be the headquarters of Lazy J.

There were two other spreads to the northwest, he knew, but from his vantage point he could see nothing in the way of buildings in that direction. Figure 2 and Bar W were probably too far up the valley to be seen even though the clear air did seem to bring everything so close.

The whole valley was peaceful and quiet, several bunches of cattle grazing idly within the range of Moran's vision, while a single rider appeared just beyond the line of the middle hills. He was too far away for Johnny to tell anything about him but he seemed to be riding from one bunch of steers to another as though making some sort of casual inspection.

All in all it seemed like good ranch country, Johnny thought, particularly when compared to the expanse of barren mountain terrain through which he had recently passed. The nearly parallel ridges offered winter protection for the stock while everywhere the grama grass seemed unusually luxuriant. And Antelope Creek was reputed to carry a good supply of water even in summer. To Moran the valley looked like better cattle country than the Arriba Basin and he knew a quick interest in it. A man could do quite well for himself in a spot like this—if rustling could be killed off.

He rode on down to the rolling grasslands of the valley, aware that he had been fooled by perspective again. He had been higher than he had realized when he paused for observation. It required quite a bit of time to reach the grasslands and when he finally broke out into the open he saw that the line of central hills loomed fairly high. They were steeper and more rugged than they had looked from the superior elevation on the southwestern slope of the Saddlebacks. Together with the still unseen Antelope Creek they formed a significant barrier between the two halves of the valley. Maybe that was a point worth noting; the hills might screen rustler operations in this half from observation by the folks across at Lazy J headquarters.

He thought about it as he rode straight for what appeared to be a low spot in the hill chain. It was still possible that the trail he had recently used was the passage for handling rustled stock. Certainly its lower reaches would be screened from cross-valley observation. The fact might have been overlooked by Rance Whitaker even though it seemed pretty obvious. Moran promised himself that he would not forget it. He had reason to remember.

He swung aside twice to glance at small bunches of sturdy-looking shorthorn steers and to study the Whitaker brand on their flanks. The Lazy J seemed to be a very simple brand, consisting only of a plain J lying on its back. There was not even a cross bar at the end of the straight shank, the whole design looking like a fishhook with its point curving upward. Johnny decided that it would be an easy brand to alter and he tried to figure out how it might be blotted into one of the other valley brands. The answer was not easy. In Figure 2 the curve ran in the opposite direction. Bar W didn't seem to fit at all. There was a small outfit somewhere to the south, he understood, which used a square with overlapping corners as its brand. Pigpen, they called it. Perhaps the horizontal J might be turned into such a square but the job would require great pains on the part of the brand blotter and would certainly look clumsy no matter how skillful the running-iron expert turned out to be. Brand blotting didn't seem to be the answer to the rustling problem of Antelope Valley.

A glance at the earmarks confirmed the belief. Whitaker's slash was a full cut almost like the old Jinglebob. It would be almost impossible to disguise by over-cropping. Any rustler who could disguise the Lazy J brand and also hide that ear-crop was a real wizard. Moran didn't believe it was happening that way.

He was still considering the angles when he climbed the pass, still unable to find an answer. At the crest of the climb he could once more see the southwest segment of valley, the Lazy J buildings looking larger and more distinct as the distance was cut down. The valley itself was still quiet and now he could not even see the rider who had appeared earlier.

Halfway down the southwestern slope he

realized that he had not seen the rider because the man had been concealed by the slope itself. A break in the trees gave him a view of the valley and he was just in time to get a glimpse of the fellow disappearing into the woodland directly below. Moran realized that he was staring down upon the tops of a long line of cottonwoods so he knew that Antelope Creek must fringe the steep base of the ridge on this side. He could not see the water for the overhanging trees but it was easy to see where the pines ended and the cottonwoods began.

Not that he was particularly interested in the point. More significant was the quick impression of furtiveness which had come to him from his brief look at the rider below. The fellow apparently had worked his way across the valley from Lazy J, checking cattle—or pretending to do so—and was now ducking hastily into the cover of the trees which lined the creek. There ought to be a reason for such a suspicious-looking move, Moran thought. And all suspicious movements were worth investigating, especially after that dynamite business.

Johnny rode on slowly, waiting until he struck what appeared to be the last sharp pitch down to the level of the stream. The trail was now angling down the ridge on a long slant, avoiding the worst of the grade. It was easy to look out across the valley now and Johnny checked his previous impression that the creek lay directly below the precipitous drop.

At one of the angular turns in the steep trail he caught sight of a clean-limbed buckskin bronc picketed at the edge of the cottonwood beyond the creek. There was no sign of a rider near the animal but Moran didn't pause to study the scene. Instead he hurried on until he was hidden behind a shoulder of rock. Dismounting there, he cut back afoot, working his way down the slope through the scrub pines which kept a precarious footing among the rocks. There ought to be some spot along here where a man might conceal himself and study the scene below. The whole affair might turn out to be unimportant but a man who had just missed connections with a man-trap was not the fellow to pass up any such broad hint as had just been tossed at him. That mysterious rider had not acted like an honest cow hand.

He quickly found that his task was to be a difficult one, the slope breaking away into what was virtually a cliff. In places he could look down into the clear waters of a creek which seemed to flow lazily across alternating pools and sand bars, the screening cottonwoods overhanging only the far bank.

He moved as quietly as possible, aware that the cliff top he was following was becoming lower as he moved along it. Some of the cottonwoods already reached above his own position and in places he could see the ground on the opposite side. But he could not spot the man he was stalking.

Working forward with due caution he saw the buckskin which he had noted from the trail but there was still no sign of a rider. Then the creek took a sharp bend, cutting around the steep slope of the ridge. Moran could see that the drop was an abrupt one now, the creek evidently having eroded a part of the ridge itself. It was then that he heard the distinct sound of something hitting the water just beyond the bend.

He went down promptly, creeping through the bushes with elaborate caution to cross the point of land which formed the inside of the bend. It took several minutes for him to get into position to see the full sweep of the creek once more but then he saw only the far side. The overhang of the bank concealed the nearer shore.

He inched forward slowly, uneasily aware that he was getting out into the open where he might be observed by anyone concealed in the brush on the far shore. Still he was determined to view the entire stream before he committed himself to any new move. He wanted to know where the mysterious rider had gone—and he wanted to know what had hit the water.

Suddenly a smaller splash sounded from the near distance, almost below his position. He tried to freeze where he was but was dismayed to feel himself sliding forward. The eroded bank must have been crumbling gradually as the gentle current washed against it and Moran's weight had caused the treacherous overhang to collapse. There was no warning at all. The ground simply gave way and he plunged headlong toward the creek.

He was conscious of a high-pitched exclamation as he sprawled through the air but then he found himself struggling in water that was over his head. Swimming wasn't easy with a .45 in one hand and a gun belt weighing him down but he came up sputtering, clawing water until he felt sand under his feet. It was then that he learned who had been responsible for the cry he had heard. Another head appeared above the surface of the water not twenty feet from his own and he was astonished to realize that it was the head of a woman. Or rather a girl. Wet hair hung partly across her face but he had a feeling that she was not very old.

"You get out of here!" she said wrathfully, her anger not unmixed with something like fear. "You . . . you snooper! You spy!"

"Sorry, lady," he choked, trying to get the water out of his nose. "I didn't know . . . you . . . were here."

"That's likely!" she snapped. "You deliberately sneaked through those bushes to pry!"

Relief as well as amusement made him chuckle

as soon as he could catch his breath. He reached out to recover the Stetson which was floating away in the current, dropping his gun as he did so. By the time he had recovered it from the sandy bottom he was willing to be completely amused at the silly way the whole affair had turned out.

"I wasn't prying, sis," he told her, still grinning. "When I go swimming with the gals I don't do it the hard way."

"I don't care to discuss it with you," she retorted, assuming all the dignity possible to a woman whose wet hair plastered her face in such dismal fashion. "Get out of here! At once!"

He decided that she must be accustomed to giving orders. And she didn't sound quite as young as she had first seemed. Even at the distance he was aware of a white form beneath the surface of the water and he knew why she was so perturbed. A girl who had slipped away for a quiet swim without the encumbrance of a bathing suit would naturally be a trifle annoyed to have a man come blundering into her supposedly private swimming hole. He smothered the grin as he looked around to determine the best means of reaching shore where the bank would not be too high to climb. "You're plumb unsociable," he complained, letting the words come out in a plaintive drawl. "To look at you a feller wouldn't figure you was half that mean."

"Then don't look!" She went a little lower in the water as she snapped the words. "Just go. And I want to hear you shout when you're well out of sight. I'm not coming out until I hear you call."

"Kinda uppity, ain't you?" he inquired. "For a gal who's askin' favors you're downright unpolite. Suppose I won't go?"

He was instantly contrite for having said it. The expression of alarm which showed behind the wet hair told him that he had not appraised her correctly. She was not as uppity as she sounded; she was scared. And understandingly so. "But quit bellyachin'," he hurried to add. "I'm gettin' out as soon as I can figure how to climb out o' this place. I never had no hankerin' for sociable swimmin' with female tadpoles what look like somethin' the cat dragged in and left under the stove."

There was a flat silence along the creek as he paddled easily across a pool to a place where the cutbank was not too high to climb. Then he hauled himself to dry land, standing there to drip for a minute before turning away. He slapped some of the water from his bedraggled Stetson and jammed it down on his head as he glanced back toward the girl. She had turned her back but his new elevation told him more about her than he had previously realized. "So-long, sis," he said cheerfully. "Mighty nice makin' your acquaintance. Let's go swimmin' again some warm day. Mebbe you ain't as tough as you sound."

Her reply was curt and to the point, made without a turn of the head. "Just go. And don't forget to shout."

"I'm awful tempted not to be a perfect gent," he drawled. "But I'm on my way. Sorry I spoiled your swim."

Walking was not a pleasant occupation at any time for Johnny Moran and he found the going doubly hard with both boots full of water and the terrain slanting so sharply. Still he plunged ahead until he had covered some fifty yards. Then he turned to bawl, "Bail yourself out, sis. I'm way over here." That done he sat down on a ledge and pulled off his boots, pouring the water out.

"Nice stunt, that was," he told himself ruefully. "I'm sure glad Old Man Barlow wasn't around to watch 'Stupe' Moran fallin' into the crick. He'd have let himself go for real on the subject of a man who hunts rustlers and runs into a gal swimmin' buck . . . Not that it wasn't a right nice change, at that."

Chapter Five

JOHNNY MORAN was in reasonably good spirits when he sent the black bronc across Antelope Creek and into the open country beyond the cottonwoods. The tension of the morning had dissolved with the unexpected comedy and he was already beginning to forget his physical discomforts. A warm sun was drying the garments which he had wrung out before resuming his journey and aside from wet boots he was not too conscious of his recent mishap. And little discomforts could easily be forgotten in the memory of a white form gleaming through crystal water. Mighty picturesque country around here, he told himself with a chuckle.

He studied the surrounding region with some care, half expecting to see buildings which had not been visible from the ridge. However, there were no houses in sight except those of the still distant Lazy J and he was left to wonder where the girl had come from. Not that he had much time to consider the matter. Almost at once he realized that another rider was in sight, this time almost certainly a man.

Oddly enough the fellow was working along from one bunch of cattle to another, just as the girl had done earlier. He seemed to be checking something or other but he broke off to ride directly toward Moran.

"Welcome committee," Johnny told himself, still letting his thoughts break out in audible expression. "Now I got to be on my good behavior so I'll impress folks."

The two riders came within hailing distance quickly enough but the cowpuncher seemed to be puzzled as he demanded, "Yuh got business on this range, bub?" The question was not exactly offensive but the man wasn't trying to make his tone particularly pleasant. Moran had a distinct impression that the question had been phrased as both a challenge and a concealment of the speaker's concern.

"I reckon so," Johnny replied easily, studying the man with a frank stare. He saw a stocky fellow of perhaps thirty-five, a capable-looking cowpuncher whose rough garb and weathered features stamped him as a seasoned hand. The brand on his bronc's shoulder further marked him as a Lazy J employee. "I'm lookin' for a Mister Rance Whitaker at the Lazy J. That the place ahead?"

"That's the place," the puncher told him dryly, still studying Moran with the same show of perplexity. "Which way did yuh come in?"

Moran waved a hand behind him. "Over the mountains. Why?"

"I was curious. We don't git many visitors. Honest ones, that is—and there ain't many trails through that country." There was still the challenge in the seemingly casual statement. It seemed clear that the man wanted to know something but was unwilling to ask his question.

Johnny pretended to miss the point. "Plumb short o' trails," he agreed. "I saw a heap o' rough country before I busted over the ridge. My name's Johnny Moran—if that means anything to you."

The man nodded grudgingly. "I kinda suspected it—even though yuh ain't jest what I had in mind. The boss told us yuh'd show up today— if'n yuh're the hombre he's expectin'."

Johnny grinned. "I'm him—even if I ain't as tough-lookin' as maybe you figured I oughta be. I even got the scars to prove it. Wanta see 'em?"

The Lazy J man seemed to relax. "Prove it to the boss. I'm Ed Underhill. Looks like yuh got some wettin' as well as some scars."

Moran pulled a wry face. "Fell in the crick," he explained. "Awful dumb of me. 'Specially when it ain't Saturday for three days yet."

Underhill guffawed, his broad face turning into a round cheeriness for the first time. Evidently convinced of the intruder's identity he seemed to lose both his truculence and his perplexity. "Real careless," he agreed. "Yuh'll git flung outa the union if yuh try tricks like that."

69

"Next time I'll be careful how I drink water," Moran told him, using the feeble joke to avoid further discussion of the true facts. "See you later. I better get on to the home ranch and report in to Whitaker."

Underhill waved a negligent hand and Moran sent the black on across the rolling grasslands of the basin. The meeting had ended on a jovial note but he had two little items to carry along with him as mild annoyances. One was the remark he had made almost at the last, the promise to be more careful in the future. It hadn't been meant seriously but it made him think of the number of times he had said something similar to XT men. Surely he wasn't going to start right in on his new job with similar promises. It was a habit he would have to break—now.

The other source of concern was not so plain. In a manner which he could not quite justify even to himself he had a feeling that there had been more behind Underhill's manner than had been explained. It was reasonable that a Lazy J cowboy should want an explanation from an intruder but Underhill's questions had not been as plain as they might have been. The man was hiding something.

Moran was almost completely dry when he approached the sprawling buildings and corrals which made up Lazy J headquarters. There was a log house which would be Whitaker's home, a rather pretentious building which would have done credit to any ranch in the territory. Fifty yards away was an equally large but plainer structure which evidently was the combined bunkhouse and cook-shack for quite a large outfit. Behind it was a scattering of other buildings of the type usually found on a prosperous ranch, while three sizeable corrals completed the lay-out. Everything was in excellent condition and Moran decided that Rance Whitaker must be a fairly well-to-do citizen. He felt a little better about having let Old Man Barlow talk him into demanding such a high wage for his services. Whitaker could afford it.

He dismounted at the edge of the broad veranda which ran around two sides of the ranch house, tying his horse to the railing. Almost at once he found a stout gray-haired woman at his side, her expression questioning.

"Afternoon," he said politely. "I'm Johnny Moran. Mister Whitaker is expecting me."

The lady seemed a little surprised—and promptly explained why. "We didn't expect so young a man," she said, her quick smile taking away any hint of disappointment which the words might have implied. "I am Mrs. Whitaker. Won't you step inside? My husband is unable to come out to meet you."

Moran had to halt inside the door, letting his eyes accustom themselves to the comparative darkness of the interior. Even as he paused a voice came to him from across the room, a sharp, almost querulous voice which demanded, "Did I hear you say that you were Moran?" It was clear that the speaker was not at all convinced.

"I'm Moran," Johnny said a bit sharply. He was beginning to be a trifle annoyed at the way everyone seemed to question his identity. Maybe that was the penalty a fellow had to pay for having a snub nose and a constant look of juvenile mischief. No one wanted to take him seriously—and it wasn't always possible to whip the fellow who doubted. "I'm Moran and I can prove it, no matter what everybody seems to think. Did you invite me over here to hunt rustlers or to look like the tough old law-dog in an opera-house show?"

"Don't get proddy," Whitaker retorted. "I just didn't expect you to . . ."

". . . to look like a youngster. All right. I've heard that before."

He broke off a bit hastily as he realized that the man across the room from him was a cripple. Rance Whitaker resembled Old Man Barlow in that he was lean, wrinkled and sour-looking. A shock of white hair made him appear older than Moran estimated him to be, but his most striking feature was a leg which was held straight out before him on a low table.

"Sorry," Johnny apologized. "I didn't mean to

sound that way. Business is business with me—and my nose ain't got a thing to do with it."

Whitaker laughed suddenly and the strain seemed to break with the laugh. "My fault, Moran," he conceded. "Maybe I'm glad to hear you talk like that. I want a man with guts enough to take charge here—and you sound like that man."

"Thanks." The interval had given Johnny a chance to see that the propped-up leg was in a splint. "Accident?" he inquired.

"Not what I'd call an accident," Whitaker told him bitterly. "The only accident was that I didn't get killed. I spotted those rustlers last week and they tried to shoot me. Killed my horse and I busted a leg when I went down with the bronc. The only satisfaction is that I've seen the thieves at last. Now I know they're the outlaws I thought and not the spooks some fools around here were talking about!"

Mrs. Whitaker had remained standing just behind Moran. Now she spoke in the same quiet tone with which she had greeted Johnny, a tone which contrasted notably with her husband's tendency toward sternness. "You're wet, Mr. Moran."

Johnny let a hand stray to the part of his anatomy which had been pressed too close to the saddle for the sun to dry. A glance over his shoulder told him that the stout lady was laughing at him so he grinned in return. "I fell in the creek," he explained.

"That's better," she nodded. "I wanted to see if you could laugh at yourself. You sounded almost as stern as Pa when you first came in."

Johnny found it easy to smile at her. She seemed like such a comfortable soul and her quiet way of admonishing both her husband and himself had been effective. "My apologies, ma'am," he said. "The only excuse is I fell overboard and it kinda spoiled my good nature. Then I met one o' your cowpunchers and he seemed right put out because I didn't look so awful mean and ornery. When Mr. Whitaker started in on the same tack he kinda hit a raw place."

"Have you got dry clothes?" she asked, tacitly accepting the explanation.

"There's a spare shirt and levis in my blanket roll."

"Go get them. You'll be better able to talk sensible business when you're dried off."

Rance Whitaker interrupted with a laugh that seemed intended amiably but which did not quite hide his irritation. "That's a woman for you, Moran. They give orders every time they get an excuse. Never let 'em get started, that's my advice . . . but you might take your bronc out to the corral before you shuck outa your wet clothes. You'll have a room in here, of course."

Moran was glad to escape from the big living

room which he now saw to be well furnished and with a definite touch of the feminine in its appointments. He hadn't quite made up his mind about his new employer. Whitaker talked like an educated man but somehow he didn't seem sure of himself—and his temper was certainly not very even. It might be a good idea to consider matters a little before getting down to business.

He turned the black into the nearest corral, hauling his saddle and gear to a building which turned out to be what he expected, a sort of toolshop and harness repair shop. Then he went back to the house, not having seen any other member of the Lazy J crew except a fat Chinese who appeared at the kitchen door.

There was only a brief exchange of meaningless remarks as he was shown to an airy bedroom back of the big room. There he changed clothing, placing the still damp boots on his feet again, for the simple reason that he had no others. Then he went back to where Rance Whitaker waited for him. This time the man was alone.

"Sit over here, Moran," the lean oldster invited, his tone more friendly now. "Maybe we can talk sense without any women to horn in. I'm kinda curious about you. All that talk in the paper sure set you up as a ring-tailed wonder."

"You can't believe papers," Moran said quietly. "I was lucky."

"We'll soon see whether it was luck or not. Got any ideas about what's going on around this valley?"

"A little. I rode through the badlands and I saw enough to make me think that the horse thief crowd that I tangled with before is the same outfit that was behind your rustling. Before I go into details, though, I'd like to ask a couple of questions. First, how many people knew that I was going to be arriving here today?"

"My whole crew. And the family. Must be about ten all told."

"They knew I was coming across the badlands?"

"I think so. It wasn't any secret, was it?"

"No. But how did you get the word from Kincaid? Did he write or wire?"

"He wrote a letter. Curly picked it up when he was in Dragoon Bend."

"Then no one in the Bend knew the details?"

"I wouldn't figure they did. Ain't nobody been away from here since the letter came." In his earnestness Whitaker was forgetting the careful grammar which had marked his earlier speech. "Why all the questions about the letter?"

"Because somebody set a man-trap back there in the Packsaddles. I think it was intended for me—so somebody who knew I was coming must have set it."

Whitaker's thin face puckered into a look of

trouble. "A man-trap!" he exclaimed. "What kind?"

Moran told him, going into some detail. When the story was completed Whitaker nodded slowly. "I guess I picked the right man," he said. "You were smart to spot it. When I first saw you I doubted my judgment in hiring you but then I liked the way you slapped back at me. This job calls for a man who has both nerve and brains. I think you're the man."

Johnny wanted to grin as he thought about the snort that remark would probably have brought from any member of the XT crew. He kept his face straight, however, as he replied, "I'll try to show you that you're right. Now let me hear about your brush with the outlaws. Did it happen in a spot where there would seem to be some connection with this trail I foolishly lost?"

Whitaker shook his head. "Too far down the valley, I think. I was out making a special check of my stock. I've got some purebreds of several kinds in the herd and that's where most of the loss seemed to fall. Anyway, I was counting noses when I spotted three riders hazin' about twenty prime steers along the far side of the valley."

"Southeast of here?" Moran interrupted.

"That's right. Maybe ten miles downstream. I rode to cut 'em off and they didn't even seem to be suspicious of me until I got close. Then they huddled for a minute and started to cut loose with their guns at medium close range. I wasn't hit, but one slug killed my bronc deader'n Santa Anna. I went over his head and was fool enough to bust a leg. Likewise I passed out cold. When I woke up the rustlers were out of sight, the cattle were still bunched where they'd been left, and one o' my men was ridin' up from the rear to help me. I guess I was kinda lucky that Underhill happened to trail me out there; I mighta been on the ground a long while if he hadn't seen what happened."

"Did he see where the rustlers went?"

"Not exactly. They disappeared into the foothills of the big ridge. A couple of the boys went over that way to look for sign next day but they didn't find anything. Either too dumb or too lazy, I guess."

"Did you get a look at the men who fired at you?"

"Not enough to identify anybody. They looked like three ordinary cowpokes but I'd figure two of 'em to be younger men than the third. They seemed lighter through the shoulders and not so sure of themselves. He seemed—the older one, I mean—to be giving orders before they started to open fire."

"Any passes across the ridge down that way?"

"Not that I know of." He grimaced as he added, "But you can't go by me. I don't even know about the trail you took coming in. My time has always been spent right here in the valley—or in the Antelope Hills; the mountains are not familiar stamping grounds to me."

They talked for a good half hour after that but Moran learned nothing more. Whitaker's brush with the rustlers seemed to fit with other known facts in the situation but it added only one meager detail. The rustlers had been driving cattle toward the southeast. That fitted with the previous guess Moran had made back there in the mountains. It was not the valley outlet to the northwest which the thieves were using. They were not working out past the Figure 2 and Bar W outfits. The trail was in the opposite direction, toward the long curving line of the Santa Fe railroad.

Actually there had been a couple of other items but his mention of them had been mostly for purposes of impressing Rance Whitaker. As yet he could not be too sure that he wasn't dreaming up ideas for that purpose. One point dealt with the way the rustlers had permitted Whitaker to ride close, not attempting to flee while there was yet time to escape any chance of recognition. When the rancher closed in they had fired hastily.

"I figure they expected somebody," Johnny said thoughtfully. "They thought you was that somebody so they didn't hightail it into the timber when they saw you. When you got too close they saw their mistake and was scared they'd been recognized. So they tried to shoot you down—

and probably thought they'd killed you when you got knocked cold."

"Sounds reasonable," Whitaker commented. "What does it mean?"

"Two things. The rustlers aren't strangers to you—and they've got a friend on your payroll."

"I can't believe that."

"It adds up—just like the stealin' of your fancy stock adds up. The only hosses they've been stealing out of the Raton Basin have been blooded animals. It points to small operators playing for big profits by stealing only the best."

Whitaker nodded his head slowly. "I think you're right. Maybe that's why I wanted to hire an outsider whose opinions I could respect. I hated to believe anything against my own crew. When you tell me I have to accept it."

Mrs. Whitaker came in while Johnny was trying to keep from blushing over that one. Without ceremony she announced, "You're both going to rest now. I won't have Rance exciting himself too much and I know that Mr. Moran has recently been injured."

"I'm fine," Johnny told her with a chuckle. "But you'd better call me Johnny. That mister business kinda bothers me."

"Very well, Johnny. Go lie down a while. Rance can stretch out in his chair. We'll have supper in just an hour. Sleep if you can."

"Say somethin', Moran," Whitaker begged half

humorously. "I hired you to give orders. Don't start takin' 'em from a woman."

Johnny grinned a little uneasily at the woman who was smiling so quietly at him. With a sudden flash of intuition he understood the seemingly odd behavior of Rance Whitaker. The rancher was henpecked, as Old Man Barlow had said. His wife ruled him in a way he could do nothing about, simply by using gentleness to get her own way. Maybe that was the worst kind of female bossing, Johnny thought. A man couldn't fight it. Certainly he didn't propose to try now.

"It kinda sounds like good advice to me," he drawled, trying to pretend that he wasn't ducking the issue. "I'd like to get my feet outa these wet boots."

"Coward!" Whitaker accused. "When you've lived as long as I have you'll know that wet boots ain't nothin' to being bossed around by a woman all the time."

Johnny tried to make his laugh sound genuine. Then he retreated to the safety of the room that had been assigned to him. Maybe this was a peculiar job he'd taken on, but his new boss was just as peculiar.

Chapter Six

H E TRIED TO do some thinking on both sub-
jects but the bed was simply too much for
him. Not in years had he stretched his lanky
frame on such a soft mattress and he found
himself blinking almost as soon as he shucked
out of the damp boots. There was a final flurry of
talk from the other room and he heard Whitaker
ask irritably, "Didn't Billy get home yet?" Then
he slept.

His next conscious thought was of Mrs.
Whitaker calling him to supper and he came
to his feet quickly, aware of several sore spots
where tense or injured muscles had tightened up.
That part eased quickly enough but he blamed
himself for not having placed the boots nearer
the open window. They seemed at least two
sizes too small when he jammed his feet into
them. Washing sketchily in the basin on the little
washstand, he slicked his unruly sandy hair into
something resembling order and went out into
the big room.

This time there were three persons present,
a younger woman in addition to the Whitakers.
Johnny saw that she was somewhat taller than
Mrs. Whitaker, her height in no way detracting

from the picture of quiet charm which she made. She wore a severely plain dark gown, but its severity only seemed to set off better the lines of a slender but interesting figure. At the same time it threw into sharp contrast the wavy hair which was just a shade off blonde. She would have been very pretty, Moran thought, if she had not seemed so stern. Her lips were tightly compressed and there was a look of sharp doubt in her eyes. For a moment he guessed that she had been engaged in some sort of wrangle with the Whitakers.

"This is my daughter Wilma," Mrs. Whitaker announced with evident pride. "Billy, meet Mr. Moran—who prefers to be called Johnny. He's the investigator who has come to see what can be done about our troubles."

Things suddenly began to add up in Johnny's head. This was the Billy he had heard mentioned although at the time he had sleepily assumed that the bearer of the name would be male. And Billy was certainly the young lady whose swim he had so clumsily interrupted. Her hair had looked straighter and darker when it was wet, but the well-cut features were the same, especially when they were set in the same severe expression. Nor was it at all likely that there would be another girl like this one in the neighborhood. Almost grudgingly he told himself that they didn't come like this one very often.

She nodded quietly, her voice cool as she murmured, "How do you do, Mister Moran?" The words were almost expressionless, but he caught the glint of challenge in the gray eyes which stared so unblinkingly at him. Evidently she knew that he had not mentioned the incident of the creek and she was waiting to see whether he would do so now. At the same time she was serving notice that she did not propose to accept her mother's hint about calling the visitor by his first name.

Johnny bowed low enough to hide the trace of smile which insisted on coming to his lips. "An unexpected pleasure," he murmured. "I didn't know that there was a Miss Whitaker."

She smiled a little as he looked up once more, obviously relieved that he had kept their secret. "My father never would have hinted," she told him with a certain dryness. "He puts up with me only under protest—and he never would admit that he had a daughter unless stern necessity forced him to it."

"Now, my dear," Rance Whitaker protested. "That's not quite fair."

"Of course it isn't," she agreed, promptly twisting his meaning. "But I don't get anywhere by protesting. You're so completely anti-female that you won't listen to reason."

"I should have warned you about Billy," Whitaker told Moran. "She has a foolish idea that she ought to be an unofficial straw boss around here. I made the mistake of sending her away to school and she crossed me up by studying a lot of new-fangled things that were never intended for girls. Then she came back here full of crazy ideas, trying to tell me how to run my business. If I'd let her poke her nose into ranch affairs, she'd have all the hands drawing their time and lighting out for distant parts."

"In most cases that wouldn't be bad," she flashed back at him. "This ranch wastes half its assets—and one of the big reasons is that you keep a crew of, loafers on the payroll. Rustlers don't cost you half as much as the idle cronies around the place!"

"That's enough, Wilma!" He dropped the air of rueful banter and became more stern than Moran had yet seen him. "I've told you that I'll not discuss ranch business with you. Certainly I'm not going to start a family row before Moran. He's not here for that."

Johnny sensed that he had seen briefly behind the curtain. Both the girl and her father had betrayed real feeling even though they had made some attempt to sound humorous with their remarks. Maybe this was a part of the reason why Rance Whitaker acted the way he did. Maybe he was resentful of feminine interference. Or was he conscious of an inferiority which he was not willing to admit?

To change the subject Moran inquired, "Speaking of straw bosses—who is your foreman? I'll probably have to depend on him for help now and then."

"I've never had a foreman," Whitaker replied. "I've run the place myself. Now that I'm laid up the men are carrying on without any particular orders."

"Carrying on!" his daughter echoed with firm scorn. "Except for chores, there hasn't been a lick of work done on the place since you were hurt. Except for Ed Underhill. He's finishing that tally of purebreds. None of the others has gumption enough to know a piece of work when they see it!"

This time it was Mrs. Whitaker who broke up the wrangle. "Johnny Moran," she said briskly, "give my husband a good shoulder and hoist him out to the dining room. Maybe some food will stop all this foolish talk."

Johnny was willing. Miss Whitaker insisted upon helping and between them they carried the disabled rancher to a big dining room where the Chinese had already loaded the table with food. There was a brief moment when Johnny's eyes met those of the girl as they joined their efforts and he saw that there was a steely glint in what otherwise might have been described as blue eyes. A spoiled darling, he decided. She had sounded like it back there in the creek, but he had made allowances for circumstances. Now he came to the conclusion that he had been right in the first place.

Table conversation was somewhat strained for a few minutes, but Johnny managed to ease matters by plunging into an impersonal discussion of the ranch and its problems. He wanted to know a lot of facts about Lazy J and this seemed a good time to ask questions. In return he repeated his story of the dynamite, for the benefit of the two women, and was rewarded by a brisk account of ranch affairs, both Billy and her father evidently trying to fit the facts into Moran's theory that the rustler outlet was downstream.

Out of it all he drew one sharp conclusion. Wilma Whitaker really knew more about the business affairs of Lazy J than did her father. That had been partly explained by the statement that she had taken over the bookkeeping of the spread, but Moran felt that her knowledge was more complete than mere accounting warranted. It made him wonder about her. Obviously she resented her father almost as much as he resented her. Both of them wanted to control the ranch, he felt sure. Could it be possible that she was working deliberately to secure such control? He didn't like the idea, but it seemed too likely to be ignored.

The thought made him uneasy. It was all too pat. The girl had acted oddly, almost furtively, out there along the creek, so much so that his suspicions had been aroused. Then he had decided that she had simply been sneaking away for a swim, but now he was not so sure about it. At the present moment he did not see a single flaw in the possible theory that the girl might be trying to get control of Lazy J by working against the father with whom she seemed to quarrel so bitterly.

There was logic behind the thought, but it was so distasteful that Moran was glad when the meal ended. At that point Whitaker made a suggestion which seemed to offer further chance of information. They were carrying the crippled rancher back to his special chair when he suggested, "Billy, there's still a bit of daylight left. You'd better take Moran out and introduce him to the boys so they'll know who he is. Likewise he'll want to know them by sight; he might need to recognize his own side before this thing's over."

Johnny made a mental reservation that he would not take too much for granted. Meeting the Lazy J crew wouldn't tell him too much about his future allies. Not when he was so sure that someone in the outfit was a traitor. All he could do would be to look them over and try to estimate them.

The girl led the way out into the early twilight which had succeeded the long bright afternoon.

Neither of them spoke until they were halfway to the bunkhouse. Then she commented dryly, "I suppose I should thank you for not giving me away. You can probably guess what my father would say if he should hear of my unladylike conduct."

He ignored the half-concealed petulance in her tone. "No thanks to me. I wasn't even sure you were the same girl."

"No? Why, you certainly saw . . ."

"Quite a lot. But the girl I saw in the water was a wild-looking kid with a mop of wet, stringy hair in her eyes. I didn't even suspect that you were a very pretty girl."

"I was not fishing for compliments—even such a dubious compliment as that one. No more of that talk, if you please."

"Don't worry. You're not likely to get any more from me. A favorable comment on your appearance is about as far as I can go. The less said about your disposition the better."

"What's wrong with my disposition?"

He chuckled at the way she had flared up. "It's too early for a complete catalog but from what I've seen so far I'd guess you'd be kinda poisonous in large doses."

"Then I'll certainly try to spare you the pain."

"Do that. I'll like it fine."

She seemed to choke back whatever additional acid she had in mind, changing her tone abruptly as they approached the bunkhouse door. She was quite genial, as she called out, "Get your shirts on, men. I'm coming in."

There was a general scraping of bootheels from within and Moran grinned at her. "So you turn on the charm for the boys, do you? Maybe your dad was wrong when he figured they'd all run out if you tried to boss the ranch. I guess you must be smarter than I gave you credit for."

"Thanks," she retorted. "For nothing."

She led the way into the bunkhouse and Moran was amused to see an elderly cow hand with a walrus mustache hastily buttoning up his levis. There were six of them in the building and the youngest was the stocky Underhill. Evidently Miss Whitaker had been quite accurate in accusing her father of staffing the spread with old friends regardless of their ability or inclination to work.

In spite of her disapproval, however, she seemed to be on excellent terms with them. There was a rattle of easy greetings and a couple of joking complaints about women invading the privacy of the bunkhouse, but she slapped back at them in what seemed to be an exchange of high good humor on both sides.

"This is Johnny Moran, boys," she announced, "the bold, brave lawman Dad told you was coming to clean up our mess. Which means he can't be as silly as he looks. Better take a good squint at him so none of you will shoot him in mistake for a coyote."

They liked that. There was a general laugh in which Moran joined, even though he caught the meaningful glance which the girl aimed in his direction. She had him foul and she knew it. Under pretense of good humor she was getting in some nasty cracks which would not permit a retort. He determined to get even for the trick.

Not that there was much opportunity to consider the matter. Miss Whitaker was making the rounds with introductions. The mustached one with the reluctant levi buttons was Curly Jeffers, the name either a reference to the mustache itself or an ironic notice of his bald pate. An oldster with a lame leg was named as Jim Glaspey, while the third one of the really elderly trio was called Buckets Simmons.

Miss Whitaker was a little less exuberant in her introduction of the others and Moran wondered why. He caught the names Jones and Toomey, but then he was staring into the rather sardonic eyes of Ed Underhill. The heavy man was grinning thinly.

"We met a spell back," Underhill said. "Just after our friend fell in the crick."

That took some of the jump out of Miss Whitaker. She almost choked, trying to ask a question which she did not quite know how to phrase. "How did you know . . . I mean, when did he . . . ?—I hadn't heard about that."

Johnny decided to haul her out of it. "I slipped when I went to get a drink o' water this afternoon. I was still kinda wet when I met Underhill and he seemed to think I always went swimmin' in my clothes."

"Oh." She had caught Underhill's casual nod and seemed to realize that Moran was repeating a story he had previously told. Promptly she recovered her poise and added, "Anyway, boys, I'm turning him over to you. Help him all you can."

"Smart hoss thief ketcher, are ye?" Curly Jeffers inquired, more than a little suspiciously.

"No. A plumb stupid one," Moran replied. "And I got the scars to prove it. A smart man would take care of his hide better than I've been doing."

Jeffers loosened up a little at that. "Got any idees about the mess we've got here?"

"It's too early for me to know anything. I'm just a pilgrim who's askin' you to fill me in on the facts."

Underhill broke in. "Yuh've talked to the boss, ain't yuh? He knows all we know. Mebbe a bit more since he had that fracas the other day. He saw the rustlers—and that's more'n any other man kin say."

"Then we're all starting even," Moran replied quietly. "Let me know if any of you pick up an idea. I'll look the ground over for a few days and then we'll get together to make a few plans. That all right with you?"

There was a general nodding of shaggy heads and he added, "I'll need someone who's pretty good at reading sign. Who's your best tracker?"

Sudden grins broke out all around him. Glaspey hitched his lame leg around toward the front and jerked a calloused thumb at Miss Whitaker. "I reckon we'll have to hand the trackin' prize to Miss Billy. She's sharp as a Comanche when it comes to readin' sign." It was clear that he shared the mixed emotions of his fellows in making the declaration. They were proud of her, but embarrassed to admit her superiority.

"I'm afraid she won't do," Moran said flatly.

"Why not?" The belligerence was back in her tone as she snapped the question at him.

"Because I was planning to take a tracker with me on a general search of the surrounding mountains. We'll be gone about three days and nights. But I'm not prejudiced if you're not."

Curly Jeffers guffawed loudly while the others fidgeted. For a moment it seemed that Underhill might step in with something but Miss Whitaker beat him to it. "An explanation is sufficient," she said with dignity. "We do not need any smart remarks!" Then she strode away into the gathering dusk.

Moran followed her with his eyes, then turned

to gaze inquiringly at the men in the room. "We seem to rub each other the wrong way," he commented. "All we've done since we met is to snarl at each other. I wonder what's wrong with her."

"What did you expect?" Underhill growled. "After what you said."

"I had it coming that time. But she's tried to bite my head off about four times so far—and that was the first time I cut in with anything personal."

"She's jealous," Glaspey stated positively. "Ever since she got big enough to stop wearin' pigtails she's been itchin' to tell folks what to do around this spread. Her pa won't stand fer no shenanigans from a gal and mostly us fellers laugh her off, bein' as we was ridin' range before she was foaled. Yuh're a stranger and she'd like to order yuh around—but yuh ain't playin' it that way. So she don't like yuh."

"Rats!" Underhill scoffed. "Yuh're makin' fool talk now."

There was an instant murmur of dissent and Moran tried to estimate the real sentiment on the subject of Wilma Whitaker. It seemed clear that Glaspey had talked for all of the crew except Underhill. The men recognized the feeling between the girl and her father, attributing it to her desire to be boss.

"That's not my present interest," Johnny told

them, breaking in. "Is it true that she's a good tracker?"

"One o' the best I've ever knowed," Curly Jeffers stated.

"Good. Maybe we'll find use for her. Who's the next best?"

"Around here?"

"Sure."

There was a general hesitation although three pairs of eyes swung toward a stoop-shouldered little man who had hung in the background all the time. The name was Toomey, Johnny recalled. No one seemed willing to answer the question and Moran thought he knew why. The tracker would be called upon for a lot of riding and these men were almost fraternal in their efforts to keep out of work. They weren't pointing any fingers at one of their number.

Moran grinned a bit maliciously, considering what might be done to get them started. "Don't worry about Toomey," he said. "If he's the tracker you might as well name him. He won't get any bigger share of chores than the rest of you. There's going to be work enough to go around."

"Who says so?" Underhill did not try to make the question sound pleasant.

Johnny looked straight at him, knowing that this was the challenge he had to expect. The crew had been given orders to co-operate with the newcomer, but they would do no more than necessary—unless the newcomer showed a firm hand in the very beginning. "Whitaker says so," Johnny replied easily. "Since he's payin' me to do some of his talkin' for him—I say so. Got any objections?"

They didn't like it too well, but he managed to put it in a tone which gave them no reasonable excuse to be surly. Underhill scowled in silence but there were nods of reluctant approval from the others. It was Jeffers who stated the official feeling of the crew. "We won't holler," he announced. "Shore we been havin' a real lazy time of it, but we ain't too proud to do a mite of work—if'n it's rammed down our throats. Take Toomey out to play Injun with yuh and tell us what else yuh want done. I reckon we're as anxious to clean up them dam' rustlers as anybody."

"Good," Moran smiled, catching the nods of agreement that went around. "Just so we understand each other. I've got to depend on you men and I don't want you getting any wrong ideas about me."

"We git the point," Curly assured him. "Name yuhr orders."

"Not yet. I'm still a pilgrim around here. I'll not ask for anything until I've had a chance to see what is needed. Then I'll come to bother you."

They seemed to like that and he went out while matters were easy. He had seen enough to feel that he wasn't going to get very energetic assistance from the Lazy J riders. His best bet seemed to be that of bidding for their goodwill in the hope that it might be worth more to him than a reluctant co-operation. He probably would get neither from Ed Underhill or Wilma Whitaker, so he would have to depend on men like Jeffers and Glaspey. It wasn't much, but it was better than nothing.

Chapter Seven

HE CROSSED the yard toward the house, aware that night had come down rather quickly as the shadow of the Antelopes fell across the valley. Over in the northeast the crinkled summits of the Packsaddles could be marked only as a blacker border beneath which no stars twinkled. A cool breeze had begun to stir across the grasslands and the whole valley had an air of quiet peace which almost made him forget that it was the scene of a particularly annoying rustling problem, one which promised to bring him to grips with men who had already demonstrated a vicious willingness to kill.

It gave him something of a start when Wilma Whitaker's voice came almost at his elbow. It was a calm voice now, almost contrite. "I'm sorry I sounded the way I did," she murmured. "I deserved what you said to me."

He managed to cover his astonishment. "Forget it," he said, almost gruffly. "I'm not here to fight with the folks I'm supposed to be working with."

She did not reply for a moment and he had the feeling that he had not said what was expected of him. "Now what?" he asked.

"I rather thought you would offer some apology."

"Why should I?"

"Because you were coarse and insulting."

"I simply answered a question."

"We'll not argue the point. I didn't wait here for that; I simply want to reach some sort of understanding with you about your work here."

"On that topic," he assured her, "I'm ready to talk. But don't try to mix any personal angle in it."

"Personal angle indeed!" she snapped. Then she caught herself. "I'll not be badgered into another quarrel. I want to tell you something before you make any mistakes."

"You're too late. I made my first big one this afternoon."

She ignored him. "Probably you won't want to believe this, but I have a very real interest in Lazy J. When I went away to school I studied every bit of scientific agriculture I could manage to get. I plugged on business methods—and I think I know why this place is not doing any better than it is. The valley is one of the best in the territory, but my father doesn't handle it with any degree of sense. He keeps up buildings and lets everything else go to pot."

"Have you told him that?"

She either did not notice the irony or she was willing to pass it up. "You heard enough this evening to be able to answer that question for yourself. My father has absolutely no respect for any woman's opinion, especially mine. He has always done reasonably well here and he's content to let well enough alone. He made no effort to improve stock until someone at Dragoon Bend put the idea in his head. Then he was real proud of himself—ignoring the fact that I'd been talking the same thing for three years. He won't make provisions for winter forage. He won't use the good bottomland along the creek for agricultural crops, even though we have to haul provisions all the way from Dragoon Bend. He keeps all those pensioners of his on the payroll, letting them laze around during the off-seasons instead of setting them to some of the dozens of chores that need doing. I get most annoyed at him."

"So I gather. You sound that way."

"Maybe I do. But I know what I'm talking about."

"Why tell me? I'm not here as a ranch expert."

"I'm telling you because I think you can help. My father seems to think you're a pretty smart man. I'm not so sure, but I'm frankly willing to use you if I can. I'm asking you to recommend a few things to him. He'll do it if you handle him properly."

Moran chuckled at her bluntness. "All cards on the table, eh?" he commented. "You don't think much of me, but you'll use me for what I'm worth. Very well. Here's my angle. I'm not sure I trust you—and I certainly don't have any reason to believe that you're the expert you claim to be. But I'll go along if you can show me that your game will help some in what I'm here to do."

"Aren't we being nasty!" she exclaimed. "But it's all right with me."

"Of course. You're figuring that it will permit you to run the place by using me as your mouthpiece. Go on with your program."

"You certainly manage to state it as unpleasantly as possible, but I still refuse to bicker. Here are two things which need doing badly. That is, they are badly in need of doing—and the men will probably do them badly enough when they get started. Just now they do nothing."

"Go ahead. Confuse me."

"I'm trying to avoid that. Anyway, there's some fence needed across an open gulley about three miles from here. Every year we lose stock down a nasty ravine, but my father has never gotten around to ordering the place closed off. The wire is ready but slipshod methods . . ." She broke off abruptly and made herself speak more calmly. "Then there's a most valuable dam across Antelope Creek about ten miles down the valley. It's in need of repair. If we don't get it fixed this summer it is likely to go out completely during the late winter or early spring. Men should be working on both chores at this time of year but my father had ordered neither piece of work done. He simply lets his old cronies draw pay in idleness."

"And you want me to prod him into giving orders?"

"I do."

"All right. Where does the other part come in? I said I'd go along with you if I could see that it had something to do with my business here."

"That's easy. You want to get information. You don't know where to look for rustler sign. Men working in two different parts of the valley can serve as sentries and at the same time have an opportunity to pick up any rustler sign which may appear in the valley. They'll be more good to you on outlying chores than they would be loafing around the bunkhouse."

"Sold. I'll deal."

"Wait a minute. There's another condition. You can't go to my father and tell him that I made this suggestion. He'd laugh at you. Be sure to make him think that you've picked up the idea by talking to the crew."

"It still sounds all right," he agreed. "But let's understand one thing. I'm working for Rance Whitaker. While he pays me it's his interest I'm out to protect."

"Why do you put it that way? Do you question my motives?"

"I question everything until I know different. Somebody around this place is on the wrong side. Until I know who it is I don't trust anybody."

"Including me?" She was clearly astonished.

"Including you. I think you're a pretty smart gal, but I'm not sure just what your smartness is leading to. Until I find out I don't commit myself."

"That suits me," she flashed back at him, anger showing again in her voice. "Neither am I sure that you're the boy wonder you're cracked up to be. Certainly you didn't seem very impressive falling into the creek. We'll take each other on sufferance. Probably it will be much better that way."

"Fair enough. Then I'll go in and suggest the business you just mentioned."

They found Rance Whitaker waiting a little impatiently. He started to ask a question just as his daughter started to make a statement. Moran beat them both to the punch, assuming all the briskness he could muster. "The crew will do," he said. "But they've got to be put on a couple of chores that'll make them useful as lookouts. Will you pass the orders to them?"

"What orders?" Whitaker was clearly surprised.

Moran explained, stating the proposition much as the girl had done. He was pleased to see an expression of relief come across the rancher's lean face.

"That's takin' hold!" Whitaker approved. "I'll get 'em in here in the morning and tell 'em."

"Give the orders to Underhill," Wilma suggested. "He's the only one with any sign of energy in him."

"No." Moran's tone was crisp. "I don't trust anybody yet. Until I know who's who I'd like to do the order passing myself."

"What do you mean you don't trust anybody?" Whitaker's eyes narrowed as he snapped the question.

"I explained part of that some time ago. And there's the matter of the jiggers who set the man-trap. Maybe one of these men did it. If we make one of 'em a straw boss we'll be taking him into our confidence. I don't want it that way."

Whitaker shrugged. "Run it your way," he replied. "I'm payin' you to handle it. Suppose I tell 'em you're straw boss from now on?"

"That'll do it. You keep me posted as to what needs doing. I'll make out to be running the show. That way I'll have a better chance to see what's what around here."

"You're appointed. Go to it."

Moran went out without even a glance at the girl. For the first time in his life he was getting something besides digs and the fact gave him confidence. It did not make him careless, however, and he used shrewd diplomacy when he talked to the men at the bunkhouse. He made it clear that he expected them to co-operate, but he didn't try to throw his weight around. Somewhat to his surprise they seemed quite willing to take on the chores he outlined to them.

"Time we got them chores attended to," Curly Jeffers growled. "We been sojerin' on the job long enough."

"Take charge of that dam, will you?" Moran suggested. "A couple of men ought to be enough. The others can set to work at the fence."

The others seemed to accept it although Underhill was clearly sulking. Either he didn't want to do the work or he resented the way someone else was giving the orders.

Moran didn't linger to spoil it. He felt that he had done a good day's work in spite of his wrangles with Miss Whitaker.

The feeling of satisfaction stayed with him while he spent a quiet hour near the corner of the ranch house, sitting in the darkness and trying to put his thoughts together. Already there were complications and he wanted to sort them out as best he could before entering upon his first day of work.

No one stirred in the open and there was only an occasional sound of movement from the ranch house. The whole place was so peaceful that it seemed like pure imagination to connect the place with a rustling problem that had already resulted in an attempt at cold-blooded murder. Or rather *two* attempts. First they had tried to shoot Whitaker and then they had tried to dynamite the newcomer.

It reminded him of the sawed-off gun which he had left in the harness shop when he moved his bedroll to the house. In the flurry of talk he had almost forgotten about it. Now he decided that he should examine it a little more carefully. Maybe someone around the ranch would recognize it. Maybe it had even been the property of the unknown traitor.

He crossed the yard in the darkness, locating the harness shop only as a darker bulk against the shadow of the distant range. No unusual sound broke the hush of the evening until he was fumbling for the door of the shed. Then he caught the soft scuff of a footstep from within. The door was open and someone was in the place, someone who was moving stealthily.

There was just time for Johnny to realize that he was in a bad position. The stranger was in complete darkness but would be able to see another person who was in the comparative light of the outdoors. He started to move aside so as to avoid the disadvantage but the move came too late. A dark shadow came at him with a rush and he went down under the charge, trying to ward off the flurry of blows that were being rained upon him. Just as he hit the ground he knew the sickening pain of a blow on the side of the head.

Then the darkness became even more complete.

When he opened his eyes again he realized that the stars were still gleaming peacefully above him. They seemed to swim around in circles for a moment or two but he didn't blame the stars for that. The ache in his head warned him that he couldn't depend on any of his senses just yet.

Finally the stars settled into place and he knew that he was on the ground at the door of the harness shed. Carefully, painfully he pulled himself to his knees and then to his feet, reaching for the door frame to steady himself. Then he went inside, fumbling for a match. Even before he struck it he knew what he would find. The slicker-roll was spread wide and the fragment of musket was gone.

Johnny blew out the match and stepped out into the night again, listening intently and trying to think it out. The odds were pretty big that this had been the work of one of the crew. It was still possible that one of the rustlers had displayed boldness enough to work into the place and take the old gun—but it wasn't likely. There was no indication that any of the gang could have known what had happened to their dynamite detonator. But neither did any of the ranch outfit share such knowledge.

Repressing a tendency to squint with the lingering pain of the blow he had taken, Moran strode quickly across to the bunkhouse door and was just in time to meet a man coming from the opposite direction. Starlight gleamed on the top of a shiny bald head and Johnny pulled up quickly, wondering whether Curly Jeffers could have been the man who had attacked him so savagely. Curly was not a young man any longer, but he was big enough and he was probably as tough as the average cow hand. That made him eligible.

"Takin' an evenin' stroll?" Moran inquired with a slow drawl.

Jeffers grunted in some surprise. "It ain't likely," he retorted. "I ain't no hand fer strolls. Got a hoss with somethin' botherin' him and I thought I'd take a look at him before I turned in."

It sounded reasonable enough and Moran could detect no trace of nerves in the explanation. "Anybody with you?" he asked.

"Nope. Other fellers all snorin' 'em off when I come out."

Johnny followed him into the bunkhouse and listened in the gloom. The proper number of snores came from various parts of the room. That seemed to leave about four possibilities. Someone in the bunkhouse had slipped out behind Jeffers, returning to play 'possum' before the bald one could get back. Or Jeffers was the man. Or an outsider had done the job. Or—and this one sounded a little stupid, even with the other grounds for suspicion—Miss Whitaker had been the raider.

Moran decided to keep his own counsel, mentioning the incident to no one until he knew a little more about his surroundings. He was still puzzling over it, however, when he awakened to a rosy dawn and it was the first thing on his mind when he reached for his clothes. Then he found something else to occupy his mind. The wet boots had dried out nicely but in the excitement of arrival he had hung his gun belt on a hook without attending to the gun. It was a stern reminder. That fouled gun represented the old reputation of "Stupe" Moran, a reputation which meant double danger now. After last night's attack he could not afford the sort of carelessness which the gun indicated. His unknown enemies were not playing games.

He slipped out of the house quietly, ignoring the sounds of activity and the smell of coffee in the kitchen. The harness shed was open and he took a quick look around before getting oil and cleaning rags from his warbag. There was nothing to give him any information on the night's prowler, so he took his materials to a bench outside the open door and proceeded to the task of cleaning the gun and oiling the leather of the belt. As an extra precaution he removed the cartridges which had been under water, not caring to depend on their waterproofing. On this job a man would need a clean gun and fresh shells.

He was almost finished when Wilma came across toward him, garbed as he had seen her when he'd mistaken her in the distance for a man. Not many women ventured to appear in levis and shirts, but it seemed typical of her that she scorned the conventions, riding clothespin style while other women used sidesaddles.

Even in the garb of a ranch hand she made an attractive picture, he decided, especially when she was wearing a smile. Then he caught himself and remembered his doubts. He would have to be careful; that smile might mean that she was trying to get her own way with something new.

"You handled everything very cleverly last night," she greeted. "My father is still talking about you this morning. He thinks you're practically wonderful."

"Smart man," Johnny told her solemnly. "I am."

"Don't let it go to your head," she retorted. "I ought to be annoyed that my father takes your advice on matters which he scorns as coming from me. But I'm trying to be practical. See that you do the same."

"Giving orders again, are you?" he commented. "Now that I'm the unofficial straw boss around here I suppose you think you're to be the brains behind the scenes."

Her glance fell upon the gun in his lap. "I'd

guess that someone has to be," she snapped. "Any man who doesn't keep his gun clean has to have someone to do his thinking for him!"

"Score one for the lady," Moran admitted. "I pulled a dumb one."

"Really? Our hero admits his failings, does he? I'm surprised."

"And tickled pink, no doubt. You seem to get more fun out of finding things to squawk about than anybody I ever met. Well, just keep your pretty eyes skinned, sister, and I'll likely give you plenty more cause for rejoicing. On this deal I'll make lots of mistakes."

She studied him for a long moment, then came over to sit down beside him on the bench. "I didn't come out here to start feuding again," she said, her tone losing its acid. "I'm still depending on you. As soon as you've had a chance to look over the valley I want you to start putting new ideas into my father's head. The part about agriculture, for example. Point out to him the advantages of combining cattle-raising with agriculture. We could save both money and trouble if we were to produce food for our own needs."

"Easy," he cautioned. "I'm straw boss for one purpose only. It's not my affair to start reforming the whole ranch. Your father probably wouldn't like it if I started getting too brash and I don't want to bust up a good situation by doing too much shoving."

"You're not being as co-operative as I had hoped."

"You set your hopes too high. I didn't come here to play segundo to your plans for running the ranch."

She stood up again, not looking toward him. "Breakfast must be ready. You'd better come along." Then she was moving away, leaving him to stare after her with some curiosity. It was difficult to remember his doubts about her when she talked so seriously about improving the property—and when she looked so completely feminine in spite of her garb. Still the doubts were logical ones and he determined that he would spend the next few days in some part of the valley not under the observation of the men assigned to the dam and fence chores. While there was a chance that she had planned those jobs to keep observers from some other part of the range he would have to take steps to the ranch house.

Sounds from the bunkhouse indicated that the crew was getting ready to set about their new tasks, but Moran did not go over to speak to them. He shoved his gun back into his warbag and left everything in the shop. Then he followed the girl back to the ranch house.

He found the Whitakers assembled at the breakfast table, the rotund Chinese bustling around as he served the meal. "Sorry to be late," he apologized. "I had a couple of chores to do. The men are about ready to set out on those jobs we talked about last night."

"Already?" Whitaker asked, evidently surprised. "You must have put gunpowder under them to get them started so fast."

"Mister Moran is really quite a starter," Wilma said with great solemnity. "It makes one wonder what he will do next." If Johnny hadn't seen the gleam in her eye he might almost have believed her to be serious.

"I'm wondering myself," he said, passing it off easily. "By the time I've had a good scout of the mountains maybe I'll know."

"How long will that take?" Whitaker asked.

"Two or three days, I suppose. By that time the crew ought to be finished with their chores so they'll be available if I need them for a next step."

"Any idea what that'll be?"

Johnny watched the girl out of the tail of his eye as he replied, "Not yet. But I think I know where the idea is coming from. Just yet I'm not too sure that it's going to be good."

Chapter Eight

MORAN MANAGED TO keep the talk on facts and figures; breakfast passed profitably as he picked up valuable information. He noted that it was Wilma who answered the questions, usually correcting vague estimates offered by her father. When Whitaker guessed that he owned ten or twelve thousand head of stock she quietly stated that the Lazy J fed a few more than eleven thousand head of shorthorns and nearly three thousand more in experimental breeds. She even broke those figures down into adult beef, yearlings and calves.

So it was with other matters. She knew exact distances, shipping rates, ranch costs and market prices. Rance Whitaker admitted that she understood such things better than he did, pointing out a little lamely that she was the ranch bookkeeper. Moran began to understand his people a little better. Whitaker was henpecked by a gentle wife because he really wanted it that way. He likewise depended on a daughter who would assume burdens distasteful to him. Then he resented both women because he felt guilty about his own laziness.

Johnny realized that he was caught up in

something too deep for him. He could sense the undercurrent of feeling but he didn't know how to figure it. Wilma knew the business and resented the way her father treated her. Did she feel a strong enough resentment to make her disloyal?

He left the house silently when the meal was over, in time to see Glaspey and Jones headed away from the bunkhouse with several rolls of barbed wire in a light wagon. Curly Jeffers and Buckets Simmons were loading work equipment on a pack horse. Underhill was saddling a bronc at the corral, apparently not intending to join either of the work details.

Johnny headed across toward the corral, keeping his voice easy as he inquired, "Which chore are you handlin', Underhill?"

The stocky man tested a cinch strap just a little too carefully before bothering to reply. Then his sour grin was faintly sneering as he said, "None of 'em."

"Why not? Got somethin' better to do?" Moran knew that the puncher was trying to bait him into anger and he took care to remain calm.

"Seems like I have," Underhill growled. "I been on the payroll long enough so I don't need to have no johnny-come-lately tell me what to do."

It was a direct challenge and Moran met it as casually as he could manage. "Maybe," he assented. "Then again maybe we better come to an understanding. What's so important?"

The answer came from behind him. Wilma Whitaker's voice was a trifle sharp as she said, "Underhill's been making a tally of blooded stock. I think he should finish it."

Moran turned, recalling that there had been a mention of such a chore. "That's all I wanted to know," he said quietly. "But I'd like it if you'd mention these things to me. If I'm to take charge here I can't have other people making the arrangements."

"The arrangement was already made," she retorted. "You don't need to let a little authority go to your head."

"Let me decide that," he shot back. "If I'm to be straw boss here I don't want interference."

He had turned to face her and now he heard the thud of a bootheel as Underhill came in behind him. The stocky man's hand came down hard on Moran's shoulder and the cowpuncher grated, "Yuh ain't talkin' like that to Miss Billy, pilgrim! Git it through yer haid that . . ."

He did not have a chance to finish his warning. Those iron fingers had dug into flesh that was extremely tender from the recently healed wound. Pain made Moran's anger explode and he wrenched himself loose with the same motion that sent a fist into action. The full right swing caught Underhill flush on the point of the jaw and the

116

man went down without even a grunt, knocked cold by the power and venom of the blow.

Moran was instantly sorry for the move, but he could not explain that pain had driven him to the action. There was nothing to do but step back and watch while Wilma ran forward to take the stocky man's head in her lap while she rubbed his temples. She uttered but one word. It was "Brute!"

Johnny turned on his heel and went across to where Abe Toomey was watching with evident interest. The stoop-shouldered man didn't look like a particularly energetic specimen but he had been the obvious choice of his fellows when tracking ability was mentioned. Toomey was not very big and his tendency to slump made him look even smaller. However, there was a twinkle in his eyes which made Moran hopeful about him. This job required a smart man rather than a big one. Maybe Toomey would fill the bill.

"We'll shove off in half an hour, Abe," Moran announced bluntly, ignoring the events of the past few minutes. "One pack horse and supplies for three days. A rifle apiece along with a six-gun. I've got my own hogleg but I'll need a rifle. While you're at it pick a good bronc for me. Mine needs some rest."

"Rifles in the bunkhouse," Toomey said, his voice thin and almost a whisper. "Yuh better pick 'em. I'll do the rest."

At least the man could talk, Johnny thought. He went to the harness shop for his outfit, bringing everything out to the open before crossing to pick up a pair of new Winchesters with ammunition for both. By that time Underhill was in the saddle and riding away to the east. Moran stared thoughtfully after him but then went on with his own affairs, giving Toomey a hand in cutting out a pair of good broncs. He threw his own saddle on a big roan with three white fetlocks, nodding approval at Toomey's choice. "Good pony," he commented. "None of your quarter horse in this fellow. You can pick 'em!"

Toomey merely nodded. It was clear that this was not to be a talkative expedition so far as the stoop-shouldered man was concerned.

Miss Whitaker appeared at the corral then. She ignored Moran pointedly and asked, "Abe, will you get the blazed sorrel for me?"

The little man moved to carry out the request but Moran stopped him. "I'll get the bronc, Abe. You go on with your chores. Get the duffle and I'll see to the pack horse while I'm at it. Got one picked out?"

Toomey paused long enough to indicate a sturdy gray. "That one," he said, still almost whispering. Then he moved away.

The girl's voice came in low-toned wrath. "Are you still trying to make it clear that no one gives orders but you?"

"Call it that if you wish." He went on to the corral without waiting for a reply. There was a flat silence until he came out with the bronc she had requested. Then he asked, "Where's your gear?"

"In the shop. I'll handle it. I don't want to interfere any more." Then she paused just long enough to warn him that she had something on her mind. "However, I'd like to ask a question—if I may. Are you expecting to meet any rustlers?"

"It's possible."

"Then you'd better fill your cartridge belt." She pointed triumphantly at the pile of equipment on the ground. "Even bullies don't go hunting outlaws without ammunition."

Moran could have kicked himself. In his haste to watch a dozen other matters he had forgotten to pick up a supply of fresh shells. He tried to tell himself that he would have noted the omission before leaving the ranch but deep down inside he was not so sure. It was the sort of thing he had done before, the sort of thing he didn't dare to do any longer.

"I don't need ammunition," he scoffed, trying to laugh it off. "Rustlers I bite."

"Now that's a brilliant remark," she snapped. "I think you're a fraud, Moran. You put on a big act of being efficient and important, but you don't even take care of your own equipment."

"Go away," he said wearily. "I've tried to play up to you as far as I could but I'm getting tired of being badgered. Maybe I could keep my mind on the things that count if I didn't have to play games with a spoiled brat who wants to be bigger than her britches."

"And I don't like your language," she declared wrathfully. "You're insulting and you don't seem to . . ."

He whirled, pinning her with a firm glare. "Look, sis! You're a cute gal—even in pants. You'd make a fine wife—for a deaf man. I'm not deaf but I *am* busy. Go somewhere else and look cute!"

Toomey came around a corner then and Moran hailed him. "Did you pick up those spare six-gun shells yet?" He hoped that would make the girl think twice about her hasty conclusion.

Abe looked a little surprised but shook his head. "Not yet." Moran was thankful for the other man's taciturnity.

"Where do you keep them?" he asked. "I'll get them while you see Miss Whitaker through her tantrum. Maybe you've got more patience than I have."

It was fully half an hour later that Toomey offered a reply to the remark. The two men were working into the hills almost due south of Lazy J, preparing to scout the region along the main rise of the Antelopes. Suddenly Toomey said, "Too

120

bad yuh got short with the gal. It mighta been better if yuh'd talked to her."

That was a lot of speech for Abe Toomey. It surprised Moran even as it puzzled him. Abe had said almost nothing since leaving the ranch but now he had put together two complete sentences. "Why should I?" Johnny inquired.

"Because she's ridin' to Dragoon Bend. I wasn't so sure it was a smart move—but it wasn't none o' my business."

"It's sure a stupid move," Moran rejoined. "Is she going alone?"

"Shore."

"Her father know?"

"I reckon."

Moran forced himself to shrug. He didn't like the idea of the girl going alone into the part of the valley where the rustlers seemed to be concentrated, but her safety was not his immediate concern. Nor would there have been any point in offering objections even if he had known of her plan. "I reckon it's their affair," he said shortly.

Toomey didn't comment further and they swung into the first real tumble of foothills. "Any trail through here?" Moran asked.

"Nope. Nowhere to go."

"We'll ride the hollows then. Sing out if you pick up any sign. We'll ride about a hundred yards apart when possible. In the notches we'll keep closer."

They had covered perhaps a mile and a half after swinging toward the southeast along the base of the main ridge when they topped a sort of promontory which permitted them a view of the valley. Moran grunted audibly at sight of a horse and rider heading southeast on a course roughly parallel to their own. "I wonder how come she wanted to go to Dragoon Bend?"

Toomey let his hunched shoulders come forward a bit more than usual. "Mostly she goes fer mail and sech."

"You mean she makes that trip often?"

"Shore."

"Alone?"

"Usually Rance goes with her. But she's jest the gal to make it on her own if she sets a mind to it."

Moran wondered why she should set her mind to it. Dragoon Bend was a good forty-five miles to the southeast. That was not the sort of lonely ride the girl would have chosen as a pleasure jaunt. Could it be that she had an errand down there at the end of the valley, an errand possibly connected with the mess which had brought Moran to the region?

They dropped down into another shallow gulch then and by the time they could see the main valley once more the girl was a mere speck along the lower extension of the line of central hills. She was making remarkably good time, Moran thought, riding hard for a person with so many miles to cover. He wondered how she expected a bronc to keep that pace for such a distance.

The puzzle of her behavior bothered him throughout the day even though he did not mention it to Abe Toomey again. For that matter nothing else was mentioned very often. The round-shouldered one didn't talk about anything and Moran was content to struggle with his own thoughts. He didn't like the way things were shaping up, but he couldn't confide in Toomey; as yet he could not be certain that Abe was not the traitor in camp.

Part of the time they rode together but once in a while they would split up, scouring different sections of the hill country while agreeing to meet at some spot which could be designated ahead. They halted for a noon rest and a bite of grub, but otherwise kept to their chore with some steadiness, not hurrying but moving as rapidly as due care would permit. It was pretty discouraging work. Occasionally they picked up the tracks of cattle which had wandered in and out of the foothills but never was there any sign of horse tracks. It seemed clear that no intruders had entered this bit of country in a long time.

Camp that night was as silent as the day's ride had been. They divided camp chores with a minimum of conversation while all talk about the day's effort was confined to Moran's doleful, "Looks like we drew blank on this deal."

On the following morning they headed south again for about an hour. Moran calculated that they had covered perhaps twenty-five miles in straight valley distance on the previous day so he was not surprised when Toomey grunted, "Pigpen's right around the next shoulder."

"What kind of folks run Pigpen?" he inquired.

"Good enough. Never had no trouble with 'em."

"How many of them?"

"Two. McSorley and his wife. Mostly hire an extra hand for roundup."

"We'll pass them up for now. I want to see what the opposite side of the valley looks like first."

Toomey simply swung his bronc's head to the left and headed out toward open country. They rode northeastward across the same kind of rolling grasslands which characterized the region closer to Lazy J. Scattered bunches of cattle gave the scene a neat air of peace, but Moran noticed that the animals varied in their brands. Some bore the Lazy J while others were marked with the rough-cornered square commonly referred to as a pigpen. Evidently this stretch of valley was a sort of border area between the two spreads. It could be a trouble spot or it might be standard procedure. Where no fences had been set up it was quite common to find cattle mingling. They would be separated without particular trouble at roundup time.

Johnny was still considering the various angles of the situation when they reached Antelope Creek, fording it at a point where its waters tumbled lazily across a stony ledge. Down here in the lower end of the valley there was no central line of hills and the creek wandered increasingly close to the sprawling Packsaddles, leaving most of the grasslands on its right bank. The geography of the valley gave Moran a few new ideas, but he was still confronted with the dilemma that had faced him from the very beginning of the trip. He was depending upon a partner in whose honesty he was not yet ready to believe.

Suddenly a possible solution suggested itself to him. "Abe," he said quietly, "I want to do some looking at this end of the valley, but I don't want to let some other sign go neglected for too long a time. It might rain. How would it be if you shoved on up through these hills until you reach the trail that comes across from the badlands? Then you could work through and take a peek at the spot where somebody got awful smart yesterday. Try to back trail the rannies who set that man-trap."

"What's that?" Toomey seemed startled out of his usual calm.

Moran studied him for a moment, then told the story of the dynamite, describing the country as accurately as possible. "See what you can find. On the way you'd better take careful note of any other sign you run across, but don't follow any other trails very far. I think I missed the boat in not going right to work on that man-trap set-up."

"What do I do after that?"

Johnny chuckled at the matter-of-fact way Toomey was taking it. For a moment the man had been startled at mention of the dynamiting attempt, but now he was back at his old habits. "I'll try to be at the dam site sometime tomorrow afternoon. Meet me there if you haven't got too far away. Use your own judgment."

Abe nodded his understanding. "Yo' goin' to take the pack hoss?"

"No. You take him. I'll make out."

They parted without another word and Moran wheeled the roan to ride down the valley once more, edging out into the open until he was riding almost parallel to Antelope Creek. There was plenty of sign there but he ignored it, realizing that this would be a well-traveled route. Probably Wilma Whitaker had covered it in her trip to Dragoon Bend. There wasn't much point in studying the traces of ordinary travel.

He found Pigpen without any difficulty. He could scarcely have missed the place even though it consisted of no more than a small log house, two decent-looking corrals, and a barn which apparently served all the various purposes for which Lazy J required several outbuildings. A grizzled man who reminded him vaguely of the XT roundup cook came out to watch as he came down along the creek, but no other person appeared.

Moran put on his most innocent grin. "Howdy," he greeted. "I'm Johnny Moran. I reckon Rance Whitaker told you about me. I'm kinda lookin' into the rustler trouble for him—and likewise for anybody else around here who's havin' the same kind o' grief."

"That so?" The old man's reply was non-committal. He was studying Moran carefully but without any hint of his feelings.

"Right. Whitaker figures it's everybody's headache around here so I'm visitin' the other ranchers. Kinda like to see how it seems to them."

"Light down and set a spell," the oldster invited, shifting a big chew to the opposite cheek and achieving quite a rustle of whiskers in the process. "I'm McSorley. Me and Rance useta be punchers together in West Texas."

Moran slid from the saddle, looping the reins around a post of the corral before accepting the gnarled old hand that was extended to him. "So I heard," he acknowledged. "Must be like old times to work this valley together."

"In a way. 'Course I ain't got the outfit Rance has. I picked up the loose pieces after he got hisself a start."

"Looks right decent to me."

"Thanks. I ain't complainin'. Rance don't shove me none. We're still right good friends and he comes by here every time he rides down to the Bend. Him and the gal both. She was with us last night."

Moran nodded. "I understood she was headed into town."

"Yep. Busts up the trip a bit if they stay over here."

"Now what about rustling? Do you lose much stock?"

McSorley shrugged lean shoulders. "Ain't got much to lose. I don't run more'n a thousand head. We figger to lose a few each year. Winter kills and the like. I ain't even sure we're havin' stock stole. Cows git a hankerin' to traipse back into the hills sometimes."

Moran stayed overnight, pressed to take supper with the McSorleys and to avail himself of the cot so frequently used by the Whitakers. It made a nice break in his chore, but it did no real good. Both McSorley and his white-haired wife were pleasant and hospitable but neither of them wanted to talk about the rustling problem. Every time it came up they switched to other topics and Moran took the hint. The only thing he was going to learn about the mess from these folks was that they didn't want to talk about it. Maybe that was significant enough. Certainly he intended to bear it in mind.

It was not until the following morning that he picked up a bit of information which started him

on a new line of thought. He had finished breakfast early, stating that he proposed to head back
up the valley to Lazy J. On the way out to the
corral he asked casually about Wilma Whitaker,
wondering whether McSorley knew anything
about the girl's plans for returning home.

The old man seemed troubled. "She didn't
seem to be talkin' much," he said. "I ain't keen
on havin' her out there alone. Them Buckalews
ain't to be trusted—'specially the boys."

"That's a new name to me," Moran said. "Do
the Buckalews have a ranch near here?"

"Kind of a one. Half-circle Bar. It's out on the
flats where these here ranges kinda sweep down
toward the railroad. They're mostly wild hoss
hunters but they keep a few head o' beef."

"Maybe I should talk to 'em. How big an outfit
is it?"

"Mebbe three-four hundred. It's a hoss ranch
mainly, like I said."

"What kind of folks are they?"

McSorley looked away. "They ain't much.
Mostly shiftless. That's why I don't like the idee
o' Billy ridin' down that way alone. She snapped
me off when I mentioned it, though."

"She would," Moran told him. "I reckon no
man gets very far trying to give advice to that
young lady."

"I didn't," McSorley agreed glumly.

Chapter Nine

JOHNNY HAD PLENTY to occupy his mind as he headed up Antelope Creek for a mile or so, turning then at a sharp angle to ride into the hills which edged the lower point of the big Packsaddle ridge. His visit with the McSorleys had left him several impressions which were not too pleasant. It seemed certain that the old man had a genuine concern over Wilma's safety—yet Moran was not at all willing to trust him. Johnny had a pretty strong hunch that McSorley knew more than he was telling.

In his preoccupation he almost missed an interesting set of hoofprints. At first they were not entirely readable but he worked back through a gulley on what appeared to be the back trail of several riders who had gone down the valley toward Pigpen. Presently he found a place where they had crossed a small brook and here the sign was clear enough. He dismounted, studying it at some length to make sure that he was not overlooking anything important. For one thing, he told himself with a wry smile, he wanted to make sure that these were the prints of shod horses.

Presently the picture became reasonably clear. Three riders had gone into the southeast some days earlier. He guessed at three or four days. In the wetter parts of the crossing the sign had become mere mudholes.

"Three men," he said half aloud. "That could be the outfit that fired at Rance Whitaker. Wonder where they came from before that? I haven't seen any tracks headed up the valley."

He remembered the sign he had noted earlier along the creek so he rode back out into the valley again, quickly spotting the marks which he had dismissed as those of casual traffic. His own trail was easily apparent, as was that of a rider he believed to have been Wilma Whitaker. The rest of it was largely up-valley traffic. Only two other sets of prints showed coming down.

"Almost slipped again," he muttered. "Lucky for me that snake-tongued Whitaker gal didn't catch me at it. She'd call me a fraud for sure."

He traced the sign for nearly a mile, realizing that he was well off Pigpen range and back on Lazy J. Then he left the creek and struck into the hills again, soon picking up the trail he had spotted before. It was not too easy to follow but he managed, presently picking up a new set of prints. Two horses had cut in from the valley to follow this sign. That would be Toomey and the pack horse. Moran could see where Abe had gotten down to study the tracks at close range, following then in the direction Johnny was now going.

At first the back trail seemed to be working only slightly more deeply into the rough country which marked the real upsurge of the Packsaddles but presently it went into a real climb, leaving the foothills entirely. It was at that point that Toomey had left it, moving on up the valley as Moran had directed.

Johnny was sorry for the orders he had given. He didn't know what Abe might find later but this was one trail which should be checked carefully. Any riders who had gone to so much trouble to climb a nasty slope must have had ample reason—and Moran felt certain that the reason was a mighty illegal one.

He set the roan to the climb, almost immediately coming to a spot where two new sets of prints cut in. Two riders had headed northwest, coming up out of the valley. The same pair had retraced their journey. It made four sets of prints superimposed upon the three sets Moran had followed.

"Still makes sense," he confided to the roan. "The first three were the jiggers who shot at Whitaker. The other pair went to set up that dynamite trap. Then they headed back past here, usin' the same trail this far. I'm gettin' warm, I reckon."

He followed the trail throughout the day, meeting Toomey in midafternoon at a spot where the hidden trail forked. For the first time in Moran's experience the little man was talkative. Toomey had spotted the trail of the trio who had fired at Whitaker but he had passed the sign, following orders. As a result he had cut back through the main pass to the scene of the dynamiting attempt and had found a short-cut from that point to the ridge trail Moran had followed. There seemed to be a clearly defined triangle of trails on the top of the ridge. One leg was the path Moran had used in reaching Lazy J, a second was the extension of the trail Johnny had more recently been following, a trail which connected the upper valley with the region near McSorley's place, while a third was a direct path across the ridge from the badlands to the lower valley, a trail by which stolen stock might have been brought across from one valley to the other.

"It's beginning to add up," Moran said soberly. "Three men shot at Whitaker when he caught 'em movin' Lazy J beef. Likely they thought he was dead or they made tracks when they saw Underhill comin' toward 'em. So they ducked out along this trail and headed down the valley. The dynamite boys used the same trail when they struck back across the ridge."

"Then they musta went right past Pigpen."

"It looks that way. Got any idea who they might be?" Toomey shrugged. "Mac works his spread alone."

It was clear that the little man didn't propose to name McSorley as a rustler even though the trail seemed to pass Pigpen—and McSorley had not reported the passage of any strangers.

They headed on down into the valley, still following the rustler trail and presently coming out near the spot where Whitaker had been shot. By that time Moran was ready to talk, all the more so because he felt that he could trust Toomey. "Might as well report in," he said casually. "I'd like to know what the boss can tell me about the folks to the southeast of us."

"Meanin' McSorley?"

"Not entirely. Mac's only one man. We know there were three in this deal, even if the two dynamiters were repeaters from the other show. Anyway I don't see Mac as the hard riders these jiggers musta been."

"Nobody else around but them Buckalews at the hoss ranch. They ain't got ambition enough to rustle!"

"You know 'em?"

"Enough to pass the time o' day—when I can't git out of it. Pore stuff."

"How many of 'em?"

"The old man and two pizen sons. Shif'less."

Johnny pursued the subject as they crossed the valley to Lazy J but got little more out of Toomey. The little man clearly didn't trust the Buckalews, but he didn't think them capable of organized plunder.

It was fully dark when they reached the ranch

house. Both of them avoided the questions of the other hands and then Moran went on to the house to make his report. Only when he had left the bunkhouse behind did he realize that Underhill had been unexpectedly civil. The stocky man had shown none of the resentment which might have been expected of him. Johnny resolved to keep that in mind. Underhill was not the type to forget easily. His show of friendliness ought to mean something.

He found Rance Whitaker fretting impatiently and the rancher's opening words hinted that the man had been worrying about something other than rustling.

"See anything of that rattle-headed girl of mine?"

Moran shook his head. "Not since she started down the valley. McSorley told me that she spent the night at their place and went on to Dragoon Bend next morning."

"She's too old to spank and not old enough to have sense," Whitaker grumbled. "I don't know why she was so all-fired set on going to the Bend now anyway. I couldn't talk her out of it." Then he broke off abruptly and asked, "What did you learn about the rustlers?"

Johnny told him in some detail. At first Whitaker showed excited interest, but then his eyes narrowed thoughtfully as he murmured, "Two points I don't quite get. You found the trail of the gunnies who shot at me, but it was their return trail down valley. How did they come up?"

"In the open, I think. Either at night or at some time when they figured the line of hills would screen them."

"And how do you think they planned to move the stock they had when I spotted 'em? You say the mountain trail wasn't big enough for a real cattle drive."

"On that I can only guess."

"What do you guess?"

"I think they would have worked along the edge of the foothills, eventually coming right out into the open."

"But they would have had to pass McSorley's place."

"That's right. McSorley's hiding something. Maybe he's afraid of them. Maybe he's in cahoots with 'em. I don't know for sure, but I'll bet he could tell a few things. Now what do you know about this Buckalew outfit that runs the horse ranch south of the valley?"

"Mighty little. They set up that outfit about five years ago. It never seemed to amount to much and we always figured they'd pull up stakes and leave. Somehow they stick it out."

"That's interesting. Stolen cattle profits might keep them going."

"But where does McSorley come in?"

"I don't know—but I'll bet he does. There doesn't seem to be any other answer."

Whitaker looked troubled. "Mac's an old pard o' mine, Moran. I don't figure he'd do anything to hurt me. Couldn't you find any sign of stolen stock being herded out in some other direction?"

"Not a sign."

"And you can't figure it any other way?"

"I might. It could be that the rustlers have gone to a lot of trouble to hide their sign, just like the horse thieves did over in the Raton Basin. They didn't hide these other trails that Abe and I were following because they didn't expect anyone to find them. They left you for dead and they expected the dynamite to get me. If their plans had worked out their trails might not have been picked up."

"That sounds reasonable."

"Reasonable—but not likely. The last part is probably true, but I don't think there has been any trail-blotting done by actual rustlers. I think they've run their stolen stock right across range where plenty of regular sign will cover it. I'm sorry about your friend McSorley, but I think he's in it up to his neck."

"But how do they dispose of the stock?"

"Now you're 'way ahead of me. As I understand it they're stealing small numbers of special breeds. That would mean a fairly small job of brand-blotting. That's the next thing I want to

137

study. It's possible for your Lazy J to be turned into McSorley's Pigpen, but it wouldn't make a very neat job. Now I want to know what that Half-circle Bar brand of Buckalew's is like. When I get an answer maybe I'll know what I'm gunning for."

The older man shrugged. "I don't like to think of Mac bein' tied up in this, but I won't argue. It's your show and I reckon you're running it all right. Make what you can of it—but don't take too many risks. We've already seen how much that crowd thinks of a man's life."

Moran smiled thinly. "I'm not likely to forget. I saw that dynamite set-up, you know. By the way, you wouldn't know who had an old Springfield musket around here, would you? I might trace the dynamiters by that."

"Sorry," Whitaker replied. "There might be a hundred old guns around the valley and I wouldn't know about 'em."

Johnny shrugged. "I'm not depending on it as a clue. Right now it don't look like we'll settle matters with anything in the way of fancy thinking. This job will blow up in our faces when the time comes. Which means we'll be a lot more concerned with new guns than old ones."

He left the ranch house rather abruptly and went out to where the hands were hunkered down in the bunkhouse, their uneasy attitudes hinting that they had been trying unsuccessfully to pump Abe

Toomey. Moran glanced around at the variety of expressions as he asked, "How much did you tell 'em, Abe?"

"I ain't tole 'em nothin'," Toomey retorted. "I reckon ye know why."

Moran nodded and perched on the end of a convenient bench. "Good man. But I reckon it's time we swapped ideas. Mebbe somebody can help us."

Abe waited in silence while Moran told the story of the dynamiting attempt and of Toomey's tracking of the dynamiters. He did not mention that they had discovered any connection between that trail and the valley. Nor did he hint at discovery of the longer trail down the ridge. He hoped that Abe was noting the censorship of the story.

"Which brings us to the point," he concluded suddenly. "There's a weasel in this outfit. Somebody's workin' with the rustlers."

That stirred up an immediate protest, but Moran silenced them with a wave of his hand. "Hear me out," he said. "The rustlers knew I was coming and they set a trap for me—just at the right time. They had to have real information from here to know that much. When I found the trap and picked up the gun lock as evidence the traitor was worried for fear it might point to somebody, maybe himself. So he stole it outa my warbag. I almost caught him at it but he knocked me over the head—likely with the gun—and got away."

There was a flat, tense silence, no man venturing even to glance at his equally uneasy neighbors. Emotions tugged at the various faces, but Moran could not interpret any of the twisted grimaces. He had hoped to spot some show of guilt but knew that he had failed.

Finally it was Jim Glaspey who cleared his throat, hitching the lame leg around in the nervous fashion which seemed to be habitual with him. "That's kinda throwin' it right in our teeth," he muttered. "Most of us have been pards with Rance Whitaker a mighty long time."

"So has McSorley," Moran retorted, letting them have it all. "And Mac knows more about the rustlers than he's tellin'. If he's double-crossin' a pard . . ." He let them fill in the thought. Then he added, "I'm depending on the honest men to help. Just keep your eyes open."

There was a deep and painful silence behind him as he went out.

Chapter Ten

JOHNNY was in the saddle at daylight next morning, striking out in a wide circle of the ranch buildings. His sleep had been interrupted by the frenzied pace of his own thoughts and he had awakened finally with the firm belief that his visit to the bunkhouse had been one of those Moran errors. He should not have let the traitor know so much. Now the fellow would be more careful.

Complete wakefulness resolved some of that feeling, but he knew that he had warned the enemy. That was why he took the trouble to make this early inspection. He wanted to know whether the warning had drawn any immediate reaction.

It had. Two hundred yards east of the corral he found a set of fresh prints. A rider had walked a bronc away from the ranch sometime during the night. It was not a clear set of prints, but the evidence was good enough. When a second set appeared close by, the tracks evidently a returning set, Moran knew that he had drawn fire. Someone had ridden out toward the central hills during the night and had returned before dawn.

He went back to the bunkhouse just in time to

find Toomey coming out. It was something of a relief to remember that Abe was to be trusted. The stoop-shouldered man had proven himself when he followed the trail which he might easily have pretended to lose. Moran explained briefly, but Abe could offer no assistance. He had heard no one moving around during the night.

"Don't ask any questions," Moran cautioned. "You might ask the wrong man and it's just as well if the polecat don't know we've got the extra information."

"What next then?"

"You'd better browse around a bit in the upper valley. Maybe it'll be a waste of time, but we can't take a chance on missing anything. If you find everything clear up there we'll know to spend all our time at the other end."

Abe grunted his agreement and they went in to breakfast with the others, nobody doing any talking while the hasty meal was consumed. It was clear that uneasiness had spread through the outfit, but Moran was content to let it go. With everybody watching everybody else there might be a blow-up of some sort that would point to the guilty man.

He left the ranch quietly, heading straight across toward the Antelope Hills on the trail he had spotted. It didn't make any particular difference that the traitor in the crew should know that his sign had been spotted. The fellow was already aware of his danger; this wouldn't make much difference.

By noon Johnny had read most of the story. The Lazy J rider had met another man near the crest of the hills during the night, probably by arrangement. That could only mean that the rustlers were keeping close contact with their sources of information. They would know that Moran had found their man-trap and that he suspected their agent within the crew. It also meant that Moran's personal danger was increased. If they had been out to get him earlier, they would have all the more reason to fear him now.

Still he took the trail of the man who had ridden in to meet the Lazy J's traitor, finding that the sign led directly toward the opening of the hidden trail which ran along the ridge. He rode hard across the open valley, only slowing the pace when he entered the wooded hills. The odds were that the rider had been a lone messenger, but Moran couldn't afford to assume too much. He didn't want to ride headlong into any sizeable bunch of outlaws.

In spite of his caution he made decent time along the ridge, finding no indication that the man had been accompanied. Evidently he had been merely a messenger.

Late afternoon found him just short of the McSorley place with the trail aiming directly toward it. Again an outlaw had not attempted to hide his passage from the man who was supposed to be Rance Whitaker's friend. Moran halted briefly, then struck out across the open valley at a place where he could use a valley swell to keep him out of sight of anyone at McSorley's. The next step seemed to be to scout the Buckalew horse ranch and he preferred to handle the matter without letting McSorley know. From the descriptions which had been given him he believed that his best approach would be from the western hills, using the cover of the southern end of the chain.

He camped for the night where the mountains broke off to become a rolling slope down to the lower flats along the Santa Fe rails. It gave him a bit of concealment for the tiny cooking fire he kindled and would, he hoped, put him in a good position to make his observations next morning. Then he made his camp a simple one and a dark one. There was nothing to indicate the presence of rustlers in this part of the country but it didn't pay to take chances. The gang he was trailing would now be completely alert to the danger they faced from Johnny Moran.

The thought was still in his mind as he watched the dying embers of his fire from the snug comfort of his blanket roll. Tonight might be the last interval of safety he would know for some days to come. It was not a pleasant thought but weariness was stronger than the sense of impending danger. Perhaps that was why he heard nothing until a voice rasped, "Don't move, pilgrim! I kin see plenty good enough to shoot."

"Shoot 'im anyhow," a second man suggested. "Git it over."

"Shut up!" the first one snapped. "Pap'll want to make 'im talk."

A heavy boot smashed into Moran's ribs and a heavy body dropped hard to pin him to the ground. He could feel hands probing for any hidden gun and then the man rolled clear.

"No gun but the ones in the belt and the saddle boot. Git up!"

By that time Moran was able to distinguish two figures in the gloom. One seemed to be tall and lanky, while the other was slightly shorter and heavy. It was the lanky one who seemed to be giving the orders. He rolled out of the blanket, obeying the sullen demand that he elevate his hands. After that they teamed up on him roughly and efficiently, lashing his hands and generally slamming him around. Finally he was boosted into his own saddle and tied fast.

"Lucky we cut across this way," one of them muttered. "Might never seen that fire from out in the open. Yuh think it's him?"

"Seems likely," the other one growled. "Let's make tracks." He had brought up a pair of broncs while his companion had been standing guard over their prisoner and now the three of them moved southward through the low hill country, the two rustlers seeming to feel their way along as though they knew the country well. Moran decided that his earlier explorations had stopped just short of an important discovery. There was something at this lower end of the mountain chain which made it familiar ground to the outlaws. Too bad he had not discovered it while the knowledge could do him some good. Certainly he was in no position to make capital of the information now.

It was not a long ride but it was a mighty dreary one for Johnny Moran. For all his precautions he was in the hands of the men who had tried to kill him without even knowing him. Now they would be even more unwilling to let him live as a menace to their crooked game.

Presently he caught the gleam of yellow lamplight ahead and his captors promptly prodded him in beside what looked like a log cabin. Voices came from the interior and one of the riders bawled, "Come out here and look what we got, Pappy!" The speaker was the one who had done the kicking but who had vetoed the suggestion for an outright murder. Moran decided that he must be one of the "pizen" sons of the reputed horse rancher.

A door squeaked open and light came out. Moran could see his captors a little more clearly but he was more interested in seeing three men crowding toward the door. Buckalew wasn't supposed to have anyone around the place except his sons. Five men were in sight now.

He had a glimpse of a bushy black beard and a narrow face which somehow brought back memories. There was no time for him to study any of the other faces. Old Buckalew growled, "Who's it?"

A burly redhead at his shoulder answered promptly—and with considerable venom. "That's Moran. Let me take a crack at him; he killed them boys over beyond the badlands."

Buckalew shoved him back. "Moran, hey?" he mused, savage humor putting a tang into his voice. "Now ain't that nice? Where'd ye pick him up?"

The fellow Johnny had picked to be one of the young Buckalews spoke triumphantly. "We was comin' across the short way. Seen his fire. Plumb easy."

"Knock him off'n that hoss. I got a few sociable words I'd like to have with the polecat. Haul him into the shack."

The orders were obeyed literally. One of the riders dismounted to untie the thongs which held Moran's legs and the other one rode close to throw a hard punch. Johnny hit the ground on his head and one shoulder, the fall twisting bound arms under him until he wondered whether his arm had slipped out of its socket. A hand hauled him to his feet and a foot propelled him into the shack where he went sprawling again, too groggy to know more than that he was aching in a lot of places.

Gradually his head cleared and he knew why old Buckalew's pinched features had seemed vaguely familiar. Except for the beard, the old man's gopher-like features were replicas of his sons'. And it had been one of the younger Buckalews who had swapped shots with Moran in the valley skirmish. Evidently young Buck had gotten away wounded.

There were five of them in the cabin now, the three Buckalews, the redhead who had sounded so venomous and the burly man who had wanted to shoot Moran on sight. All five were dirty and unshaven—and all five were staring sourly at their prisoner.

It was one of the younger Buckalews who broke the brief silence. "It's Moran, all right," he agreed. "I seen him at the old hideout. Yuh want I should bust him up, Pappy?"

The old man shook his head. It seemed clear that he was the real boss of the outfit. The others even seemed to fear him a little and Moran knew why after he had a good look at the piercing black eyes of the oldster. Buck was a little crazy, he thought. But he was foxy at the same time.

" 'Stupe' Moran," the old fellow cackled. "We just been hearin' about yuh." He turned partly toward the pair who had brought in the prisoner. "I reckon yuh didn't know about that part," he explained. "Red was down to the village today and he got quite a yarn. This here Moran ain't the smart alec we figgered he was. Over across the hills they tell it that he was plain dumb when he blundered on to the hideout. We didn't need to be worried about him—and it kinda turned out that way. Leastways he fell into our hands easy enough."

There was a general rattle of talk then as the surly man referred to as Red told the story of "Stupe" Moran and the other pair related the details of his capture. The latter two seemed annoyed to find that they had outwitted only a notorious blockhead instead of a smart lawman.

"Don't take on, boys," the old man consoled. "Fer a dumb critter he ain't been missin' too much. I heard from Soapy this mornin' and it seems Moran picked up the trail across the ridge. Abe Toomey knows about it too."

"Where's Squint?" one of the Buckalews asked. Moran found it difficult to tell them apart although he didn't think they were twins. They had the same narrow features he had noted in the old man but presently he saw that one was a little bigger than the other and had a couple of missing front teeth.

"Squint's ridin' again tonight," the old man explained. "I reckon I was too hasty. I sent him

149

up to tell Soapy not to worry, that this Moran was just a lot o' talk. If I'd waited we coulda sent word about what we're goin' to do with the damfool."

By that time Johnny had the uneasy feeling that they were discussing him as though he were not there, as though he no longer existed. It came as no great shock to hear the redhead comment, "Oughtn't to be no fuss about that part. We'll plant him good and deep and nobody needs to know nothin'."

The old man's upper incisors came out over his lip as he aimed a shrewd grin at Moran. "I ain't figgerin' that way, fellers," he said slowly. "Maybe it'd be fun to jest git even fer the boys he shot—but I been thinkin' that we could make somethin' else outa this. It's time Rance Whitaker hauls in his horns a mite and this oughta be the time to give him a gentle hint." The man was keeping his voice low now, almost gentle, but there was an underlying tone in it which made Moran want to shiver. Old Buckalew was practically a madman.

"Take f'rinstance a hangin'," the old outlaw continued, his mild tone belying the wild light in his eyes. "Wouldn't Whitaker kind a be sorry fer takin' steps against us if he found this Moran jigger hangin' to one o' them cottonwoods back o' the Lazy J corral? Jest to make sure he didn't miss the real idee we'd git Squint to write a note to hang on Moran's shirt. Squint kin write real good."

"It's a lot o' trouble and risk just to get rid o' the polecat," Red grumbled.

Instantly Buckalew whirled on him. "I'll tell ye what to do! We'll hang this critter as a warnin' that we ain't takin' no foolin' from nobody!" From a pitch of frenzy the voice dropped back into a wheedling tone that was almost worse than the rasp. "Was anybody plannin' to argue with me?"

A chorus of negatives told Moran a lot about the gang which had captured him. They were intensely afraid of the old man—and he didn't wonder that they should be. There was a tense and poised malevolence in the old man which was enough to make the toughest outlaw uneasy.

Suddenly the tone changed again, its abruptness suggestive of the mental and emotional instability of the man. Buckalew was still bossing his crew, but now he was doing it shrewdly, without threats. "We'll git right to work," he decided. "At daylight, Red, Timmy, Jake and me will git over to the hole and shove them steers fer the rails. Meanwhile Tom kin start up the valley with Moran. It'll be better to move the critter up to the hangin' in daylight. Won't be so much trouble watchin' him that way. We'll foller after we git rid o' the shipment."

One of his sons nodded grimly and the old

151

man uttered a sharp warning. "And don't ye be gittin' no brash ideas about killin' him fer yerself, Tom! This'll be a real hangin'. I'm kinda lookin' forrard to seein' him kick on the end of a lariat."

His son's glance dropped. "Where do I meet ye?" he grumbled.

"Where the trail hits the valley. Wait till we git there, mind ye!" Then he added, "Don't pass Mac's place. The old fool's gettin' scared already and he might cut up a mite if'n he knowed we was plannin' a hangin'."

They kicked Moran back against the wall then, ignoring him as though he no longer rated a second thought while they settled the other details of the next day's program. It gave him time for thought—and none of the thinking was pleasant. He had blundered once too often. This time he was to pay for his mistake with his life.

He slept fitfully during the night but felt more dead than alive when daylight brought a stir to the cabin. There seemed to be cramps in every muscle that was not already bruised and the steady pain accentuated the feeling of hopelessness. Even if he should find some way to get free during the ride up the valley he would be in no position to do anything. The physical beating he had taken would cripple him for any kind of action.

They lashed him to his own saddle as soon as they had eaten breakfast, giving him nothing at all, and then the four who were to handle the vaguely mentioned cattle drive rode away toward the rolling country at the south end of the Antelopes, the only reference to Moran being a renewed warning from the old man about not killing the prisoner too soon. It was clear now that the hideout for stolen stock was somewhere beyond those western hills but the information had come too late. The victim of a hanging would never be able to use the facts.

Tom Buckalew seemed to be in no hurry to start out. He took care of a couple of chores while Moran sat helpless in the saddle, trying to find some position in which he could get a minimum of comfort. Then the outlaw killed time doing nothing until Moran began to wonder about him. It seemed clear from his actions that he was up to something with this delay but it did not seem to make sense.

Finally they started out, Buckalew taking Moran's bronc on a long lead rope as though trying to make sure that the helpless prisoner could not get close enough to start anything. No word was spoken but it quickly became clear that the rustler still had something on his mind. He kept turning around to look back, the queer light in his eyes warning Johnny that the old man was not the only crazy one in the family. The son seemed to be infected with some of the same madness. Obviously he was planning something but it didn't seem that the plan included Moran. When Buckalew looked back he didn't even see the prisoner who rode so helplessly in his wake.

They passed several bunches of decent-looking cattle and Johnny found himself studying the brands, even though he didn't hope to make anything of what he saw. The Half-circle Bar was a rather large brand which looked something like a derby hat, the long bar crossing the opening of the half circle and extending beyond it to form the hat brim. A bit of work with a running iron might readily turn a Lazy J into a Hat. One side of the brand would probably show the alteration but the blotting might pass unnoticed if false brands were mixed with real ones.

The earmark was not so easy. Buckalew's outfit earmarked cattle with a double nick. It could not possibly cover the long slit of the Lazy J. Moran found himself wondering about it but then he thrust it from his mind. There was no point in hunting for an answer which would be useless— and a dead man couldn't use answers.

Within the hour they were far enough to the north so that hills rose on either side. McSorley's place would be perhaps ten miles ahead but still Buckalew didn't make any attempt to strike out toward either range of mountains. He led the way straight through the valley and Moran found himself wondering. His captor might be just crazy enough so that he would do something to give the prisoner a chance. At any rate the thought was a pleasanter one than the mere acceptance of aches and pains.

The trail passed a sort of gulley where cotton-woods fringed a small stand of stunted pines. It was the only real bit of cover in that part of the valley mouth and somehow Johnny wasn't surprised when Buckalew took both horses into the timber. The outlaw dismounted, saying no word to the uncomfortable prisoner but striding quickly away as soon as he had tied his own mount to a tree.

Hope stirred anew in Moran and he put stern effort into an attempt to work his hands free. No one had looked at his bonds since the previous night and now he knew that they were just a little loose. There was a certain amount of slack which he could feel even with hands and wrists that were almost numb. Flexing his fingers into an attempt to get some circulation started he fought back the agonies which the movements caused, steeling himself to continue with the effort. Pain now might mean a longer life.

Twice he saw Buckalew moving about at the edge of the trees but two hours went by with no change in the situation. Cramps were biting into Moran's thighs now but he gritted his teeth and went on with his dogged attempt to make his finger tips curl toward the knots which held his wrists. Three times he felt that he was

155

on the verge of some sort of success but on each occasion the numbness came back and he had to work to restore circulation. By now the succession of bitter disappointments almost made him forget the aches which kept him dizzy.

Suddenly he heard the crash of brush as Buckalew came running toward him. The madness was in the fellow's eyes clearly enough now but he did not even look at Moran. He untied his horse, first transferring the lead rope to the tree which had served as hitching post. Then he rode out toward the trail, leaving Moran to wonder.

Again opportunity seemed to be beckoning. Johnny forced himself to a renewed effort, getting broken fingernails into a knot and sweating at it until his whole body ached with the effort. He could feel something give a little but then the cramps caught him again and he made himself relax. It was at that instant that he heard a woman's muffled scream.

So that was the meaning of Tom Buckalew's stealthy performance! The fellow was shirking his appointed duty in order to lay an ambush for Wilma Whitaker. Probably he knew enough about her trips to Dragoon Bend so that he had counted on her returning today.

Moran went back to his desperate efforts, gritting his teeth with the physical effort and the mental determination to ignore everything else until he could accomplish something of importance with these knots. He could feel another slight loosening but his wrists were still firmly caught.

Then he heard the approach of two broncs and looked up to see Buckalew coming back with a firm grip on the bridle of Billy Whitaker's horse. The girl had a lariat about her waist but it seemed clear that she had not surrendered without a struggle. Buckalew's weasel features bore two angry welts where she had cut at him with her quirt. It was the only part of the scene Moran could view with anything but dismay.

At the same instant the girl saw Johnny sitting there in the saddle. The sight was but a momentary one as Buckalew cut back deeper into the pines, not actually passing the spot where Moran watched. No word was exchanged but Johnny caught the expression of mingled fear and disgust in the girl's face. Suddenly he knew that part of it was for him. She had not seen him clearly enough to know that he was helpless.

Working with frenzy now he went back at the knots, spurred on by the sound of crashing brush as Buckalew halted some fifty yards back in the timber. Evidently the girl was giving him a battle as he tried to drag her from the saddle.

157

Chapter Eleven

JOHNNY MORAN'S MIND was never quite clear about the precise details of the next few minutes. Anger, fear and desperation were battling against pain, exhaustion and cramps, the resulting mental state being something between confusion and a complete faint. Johnny knew that there was more freedom for his wrists and fingers now so he concentrated on that, working grimly until suddenly his arms swung back to his sides.

For some moments he could not control either of them but then he found that he could bring them in front of him, the right one reasonably sound while the left was pretty much dead weight. He didn't bother to untie the bit of raw-hide which was still on the left wrist. Instead he concentrated on bending down to get at the thongs which bound his ankles. Each movement came automatically, desperation driving him to actions he scarcely knew about as the sounds of violent conflict still came from beyond the screen of trees.

He spent another agony of time in getting rid of the final bonds and then he fell headlong to the ground, unable to use his legs any more than he could use his left arm. There was an instant in which senses wavered toward the final fringe of darkness but he fought for control, gradually pulling himself to his knees as he regained his senses. Maybe it was ridiculous for him to drag himself toward a fight in his present condition but he knew that he was going to do that very thing. Billy Whitaker needed help. Maybe Johnny Moran wouldn't be much good but he might turn the tide.

The first painful moves brought restored circulation and he ventured to get his feet under him, wavering dizzily as he stood erect for a moment before lunging forward. In that moment a gun boomed sullenly from directly ahead of him. There was a curse, the sound of a heavy fall, and then the renewed scramble of feet as the struggle went on. Buckalew's savage curses indicated that the fellow was having his hands full.

Moran heaved himself forward, keeping his balance with an effort of will as wobbly legs refused to do his bidding. He broke through the screen of pines and found himself staring at a strange scene. Billy Whitaker and Buckalew were battling for the possession of a gun which still smoked in the girl's hand. On the ground beside them a horse threshed in evident distress. In spite of his numbed perceptions Johnny Moran knew what had happened. Somehow Billy had gotten hold of the outlaw's gun. He had

159

diverted her shot and the bronc had taken the slug.

He forced himself into renewed movement but was just too late to be of any use. Buckalew saw him coming and put a furious drive into securing possession of the gun. His effort was successful but in his haste he caught a spur in a projecting root and went over backward, directly into the whirl of threshing hoofs. There was a thud and a grunt, then the man lay quiet as he fell just far enough away so that the horse did not hit him again.

Out of the tail of his eye Johnny saw the girl sink to the ground but he ignored her until he had staggered across to secure the fallen six-gun. The solid gun butt in his hand made the numb fingers feel better and he took another two steps to fire a slug into the brain of the injured bronc. Only when that act of mercy was complete did he look at the fallen outlaw.

By that time Billy was on her feet again, clutching grimly at the torn front of her shirt. "Is he dead?" she asked, her voice quivering.

"Afraid not," Johnny replied, finding his own tones thick as his battered lips and swollen tongue tried to form syllables. "Got a good kick though."

She seemed to realize his condition for the first time. "What happened to you?" she asked.

He told her, as briefly as possible. "Reckon I

didn't get loose in time to be much help. You and the bronc teamed up mighty good."

She seemed to be puzzled even as she steadied herself to listen. It was clear that she was battling to shake off the effects of the fright she had just had and he decided that it would be better to force her into some action before shock could make itself felt.

"Better go back there and get my bronc. Then you can catch your own."

She looked around in surprise as though suddenly realizing that her own pony had bolted during the fight. Aiming a little nod at Moran she hurried away through the brush. He watched her for an instant, then turned to the work of making certain that Buckalew would not recover and cause more trouble. The man had taken a hard knock on the side of the skull but it would be better to play safe with him. He might still be more than a match for a woman who was on the point of fainting and a man who might collapse at any moment.

The remnants of rawhide which still dangled from Moran's wrist were quickly transferred to the outlaw and then Johnny breathed a little more easily. Movement had chased most of the cramps and although he still ached all over he decided that the worst was past. From now on he would take care of himself.

With a bit of effort which brought renewed

aches he took the outlaw's gun belt, buckling it around his own waist and reloading the weapon which he had thrust into the waistband of his pants. Then he worked a carbine out from under the body of the dead horse and turned to face the returning Billy. One glance at her face told him that she was getting back to normal.

"You'd better give me a hand," he greeted abruptly. "I ain't in what you might call the best o' shape. Help me get this jigger's bedroll and other gear onto my hoss."

She dismounted at once, lending a hand as directed and asking her questions as she worked. "What do we do with him?"

"We leave him. Can't do much else. If he lives he'll manage to walk home—but not in time to set anybody on our trail. The jasper we got to look out for is another one o' the gang who's likely to be comin' down the valley. I didn't quite get the straight of his plans."

Her frown showed that she didn't quite understand but she confined her question to the more practical points. "Who's going to chase us?"

"The Buckalew gang. They can't afford to let me get away. They don't know about you but that won't make any difference. Got a canteen on your saddle? The polecats didn't give me a drink all the time I was their guest."

A drink of the tepid water she offered made him feel a little better and within a matter of minutes they were heading up the valley, the girl preoccupied with her efforts to repair the damage to her clothing. Moran was content to ride in silence, trying to think things out even as he forced himself to ignore the aches and pains which made every jog of the horse a torture.

Presently he said, "We'd better swing hard to the left. It'll be better if McSorley don't see us. They'll ask him and he'll be better off if he don't have to lie—assumin' that he would."

"I was planning to stay there overnight."

"Change the plans. We can't afford the luxury."

To his surprise she didn't argue. "I wasn't looking forward to it with any pleasure. I've learned things about McSorley."

Once more they rode in silence and Moran began to realize that the girl's evident curiosity was not as strong as some other emotion which was keeping her quiet. At first he figured it to be the natural reaction from her narrow escape, but then he caught a couple of sidelong glances which told him that she had something on her mind that was more than mere feminine shock. Even under the stress of fear and horror Billy Whitaker was quite capable of working out her own plans. Johnny wondered what sort of plans they might be.

Riding under cover of the Antelope foothills they made good progress through the middle of the day, neither of them speaking except for an occasional word about the trail. A little beyond midafternoon, however, Johnny knew that he had almost reached the end of his stamina. "I'm done in," he declared shortly. "If I don't get down mighty soon I'll fall outa the saddle. How far past McSorley's do you figure we are?"

Her reply was prompt. "Six miles. Hold out another ten minutes and we'll strike a brook. We'll rest there."

He grimaced. "Don't say I didn't warn you if you have to drag me the last quarter mile."

"I'm warned," she retorted. "Shall I tie you to the saddle?"

He shook his head and they went on again. Her prediction proved sound and presently Moran was sliding almost helplessly to the ground beside a clear stream which came down from the hills to wind out across the valley. The cold water helped to revive him and he lay flat on his belly for several minutes, letting the water take some of the pain out of his swollen wrists.

The girl did not comment until she had taken care of both ponies. Then she squatted down beside him to look at the broken fingernails and raw, welted wrists. "Are you that bad all over?" she inquired.

He rolled over, looking up to see real concern in her eyes. The sight bothered him for some reason he could not have explained and he growled,

"I'm all right. Got any grub with you? The Bucks didn't think I needed any."

She stared at him for just a moment, her lips tightening, and he saw that he wasn't the only one to have come out of the day with marks of conflict. The girl was going to have a fine black eye. It made him sorry he had sounded so gruff but there was no time for him to mend the bad manners. She turned away quickly, her voice carrying an edge as she said, "Sometimes I could think the Bucks had good ideas."

She came back quickly with food that had obviously been brought from Dragoon Bend as lunch for the journey. Moran accepted it with a word of thanks, eating then in silence as he found that a bruised jaw cramped his style quite a little. It was Billy who broke the uneasy silence.

"Did you learn anything about the rustling while the Buckalews were holding you prisoner?"

"A little. They're the rustlers, all right. The man who helps 'em from the inside at Lazy J is called Soapy. Know any of the hands whoever carried that nickname?"

"Never heard it before. Did you pick up anything that would serve as evidence against them in court?"

"I reckon not. It'd be my word against theirs— and they'd outnumber me. All I know is that they got a hideout fer stolen stock over to the west of the ranch somewhere. Seems like it's

165

been the collection depot fer rustled beef from quite some distances. Buckalew was part o' the gang that I tangled with in the badlands a month ago."

She glanced at him oddly. "I've been hearing more about that," she said, her tones a trifle sharp. "I went on the train to Sawmill Springs. I talked with a man named Kincaid who publishes a paper there. I also talked with two or three others who didn't share Kincaid's high opinion of you."

"Sounds like you mighta been listenin' to Old Man Barlow," he grinned.

"Exactly. When I called you a fraud the other day I didn't know how right I was. You came here posing as an expert at catching rustlers— when really you're just a blunderer who turned a stupid mistake into a lucky accident."

He tried to ignore her severity. Still smiling, in spite of the sore jaw, he commented, "Now you're talkin' like yourself. Plain poison. What makes you think you oughta believe Barlow instead of Kincaid?"

"Because Barlow's story fits you exactly. The man Barlow described is the same man who forgot his cartridges, who forgot to clean his gun, who fell overboard when he was playing Indian, who got himself captured the first time he started to close in on the rustlers he was hunting."

"Better get in the part about me not bein' able to help you when Buck was givin' you a hard time." He made the suggestion sound mild but there was a certain bitterness behind the words.

She nodded. "I'm not blaming you for that—but it does seem to fit the pattern. You managed to take a hand just when you were not needed." Then she paused before adding, "Not that you'd have been much good in a fight; you were too badly beaten already. Maybe that's the way with you, Moran. You don't use your head for much but you've got lots of nerve."

"Thanks. It's not much, of course, but it's better'n most of the things you say about me."

"I didn't intend to be complimentary. What I'm pointing out is that I am now in a position to give my father quite an account of the man he hired. I don't think he'll be at all pleased to learn that he was hoodwinked into thinking that he was getting a smart man."

"Thanks again. But I didn't ask for the job. Remember that."

"I know. But it won't make dad feel any better to learn that he hired a man called 'Stupe.' "

"Then don't tell him."

"I won't—if you'll follow orders."

"What's this? Blackmail?"

"You may call it that." Her tone was prim now, almost smug. "I've already explained about why

167

I want to make certain changes in Lazy J. Now that father is willing to listen to you I can see a way to get him to do what I want—through you. So I'm calling the tune. That's clear enough, I think."

"And if I don't play your tune you tell him all about what a chump I am, eh?"

"That's the idea. And don't try to laugh it off. I'm mighty serious about the whole thing."

"So serious that you're forgetting the rustling business and how tough a spot we're now in?"

"I'm forgetting nothing. While I was investigating I learned a number of other things. Months ago I decided that the Buckalews were at the bottom of all the trouble but I couldn't see how they managed to run stolen beef out of the valley without McSorley knowing. When you came to Lazy J I had hopes that you would straighten out the mess. Then I discovered that you were not to be depended upon. That was when I decided to ride down to Dragoon Bend and do my own investigating."

The severity of her tone almost made him laugh. In spite of his aches he could still find humor in the situation and it pleased him to goad her a little. "You're just prejudiced because I caught you in swimmin'," he said.

She did not look toward him. "Don't try to change the subject. I looked up shipping records at Dragoon Bend, Sawmill Springs and Pecos, the three nearest stations on the Santa Fe. Half-circle Bar has shipped nearly three thousand head in two years!"

"That's interesting," he commented. "They're not even supposed to be a cattle outfit."

"And I think I know how they do it. They're brand-blotters. That big hat-shaped brand can cover a Lazy J so it'll scarcely be noticed. We should have realized it sooner."

"Maybe I ain't the only stupid one," Moran murmured quizzically.

She ignored him. "My father's carelessness has played directly into their hands. They could blot the brand but they couldn't have done much about our earmark—but father didn't earmark half of our stock. The rustlers simply picked unmarked beef."

He grunted with interest, blaming himself for not having seen the point. "Where does McSorley fit in?" he asked.

"I found that out too." She was openly triumphant as she explained. "Mac was arrested about ten years ago in El Paso for a killing. The only witness was a man named Buckalew. A lot of folks thought Buckalew was lying but his evidence got McSorley off."

"I get it. Buckalew has some kind of hold over Mac. He has been using that hold to make Mac string along with the rustler outfit. Is that the way you figure it?"

"Exactly. It all fits with what you've overheard, doesn't it?"

"Nothin' to contradict it," he assured her. "So what's the play?"

She stared sharply. "I told you. I'm supplying the brains and you're to use your influence with father. Between us we clean up the ranch and break up the rustlers—or I talk. Does that sound enough like blackmail to impress you?"

"Take it easy. You've been letting your imagination run away with you. I'll play along with you to guard my guilty secret, but you're not thinking straight on this rustler deal. Just knowing the facts don't get us out of the woods. So far we can't prove a thing—even if we could find a way to make a court case of this. And right now we've got to figure it another way. Pretty soon young Buckalew's goin' to report in and we'll have the gang on our trail. They'll make an effort to shut us up before we can talk too much."

"Then we'd better get on our broncs right away." She was rising as she spoke, widened eyes indicating that she realized the truth of what Johnny had said.

Moran shook his head, remaining prone. "Not me. I'd fall off if I tried to ride another mile. You know the valley. Head for Lazy J and report in. But be careful what you say until we find out which one is the jigger the outlaws call Soapy.

I'll camp here until I shake some of the aches out of my carcass."

She studied him as he spoke, seeming to notice his real lameness for the first time. Evidently she had been so much occupied by her own thoughts that she had not quite realized the extent of his injuries. Suddenly she came toward him, her face stern. "Take your shirt off," she ordered.

"Gosh. How come?"

"Don't ask questions. I'm giving the orders now—Stupe."

He worked slowly and painfully out of the shirt, disclosing the angry brush burns and bruises which covered his ribs. "Nothin' to be done about it," he complained. "It'll heal up in time."

"Wrap up again," she ordered. "I'm staying with you until you're fit to ride."

"But we don't gain any time that way. You could . . ."

"Don't argue with me. We're camping right here until you've had a few hours of rest. Nobody will bother us in that time. Then we shove on up the valley. We can outride 'em if we have to."

He stared at her wonderingly for a moment or two. Then he murmured quietly, "I reckon you're right—even if you do have to sound so bratty in the way you put it."

"Keep the personalities out of this."

"You're a fine one to talk! You just called me 'Stupe' but you flare up when I remind you of

171

the kind of a spoiled brat you are. It ain't fair."

She laughed suddenly. "You're not just stupid," she told him slowly. "You're an absolute idiot!"

"Thanks. You're kinda cute too—'specially with wet hair in your eyes."

She swung away briskly. "I'll unsaddle and get you the saddle blankets. Nothing like plenty of heat for sore muscles. Stay quiet now or I'll take a club to you."

He grinned silently as she moved away. In some respects the brat seemed like a real good kid.

Chapter Twelve

MORAN fell asleep while the girl was unsaddling her bronc. It was almost as though the brief flurry of banter had used up his last reserve of energy. One moment he was grinning amiably at his busy but angry companion, the next he was snoring.

It was dark when he awakened to the touch of a hand. He started up quickly but sank back with a grunt as bruised muscles protested painfully.

"We'd better be moving," Billy Whitaker's voice came softly. "It'll be daybreak in another hour or so."

"I can't move," he told her flatly. "I'm crippled."

"Nothing of the sort!" she snapped. "Get up and stop whining. You'll be all right when you've moved around a little."

He groaned, testing an arm and shoulder which seemed to be one big ache. "I'll probably die before I get limbered up," he predicted dolefully.

"It's your choice," she told him, moving away as she spoke. "I'm leaving before there's daylight to show our trail to the Buckalews. You can stay here until they show up to kick you around some more."

"I'm comin'," he grumbled. "Even though I ain't sure that Buckalew boot toes are any worse than a woman's tongue."

She did not make a reply and he stamped around a little, shaking off some of the pains as circulation returned to his arms and legs. Now that he was up he decided that he wasn't going to die after all. There were not many places on his body which did not have some sort of abrasion or welt but he was steady again and he had the use of arms and legs once more. At the same time his head felt clearer. Which was good. This situation needed thought as well as action.

They saddled up in silence, breaking the cold camp without ceremony. Moran let the girl lead the way until they swung out of the foothills to take temporary advantage of the easier travel in the valley. Then he began to talk, telling her of the things he had learned, particularly about the mountain trails. She let him go on until he indicated that he had given her the full account. Then she asked, "Why didn't you tell me this yesterday?"

"You didn't give me a chance. All I could do was listen."

"Now don't start any of that!"

"I'm not starting anything. I just told you the truth. Yesterday you were so full of ideas that you didn't give me a chance to show you that I'd picked up a few things beside bumps."

"So now you're letting me see how smart you are?"

"Call it that. Mainly I'm telling you because you ought to know. I'm not going on to Lazy J with you."

"Why not? Where are you going?"

"Across the valley to the Packsaddles. As things stand we don't have any plan to use against the rustler outfit. We know what they've been doing but we're in no position to prove much. At the same time they're in a bad spot because I got away from 'em. So they'll make some kind of a move—and they'll likely make it pronto. I want to be in a position to watch 'em."

"Like you did before?"

He ignored the irony in her voice. "I'll try to be a bit more careful this time. But there's another point. This traitor at Lazy J could be the man whose evidence might wrap up the gang for us. We've got to find out who Soapy is."

"How does your trip to the Packsaddles figure in that part?"

"I'm not sure—but I've got a hunch. Think about it this way. Soapy has been in touch with the rustler messenger so he thinks that I'm a prisoner of the Buckalews. I don't think they can have passed any word to him since I got away. If I turn up at Lazy J he'll likely slip away. If you go in alone he'll figure that everything at Buckalews is just like it was. Maybe

175

he'll do something that'll give the game away— or maybe we can trap him and make him talk."

"How can we do that when we don't know who he is?"

"That's the trouble with the whole mess. We don't know the things that will help us much. All I can figure is that we'll have to play it smart and quiet and hope that the enemy will make the next mistake. You handle the ranch end and I'll take the sentry duty on the mountain. One of us might come up with something."

She was silent for several minutes. Then she murmured a dubious agreement. "I can't think of any better plan. Do you have any other ideas?"

"A few. Don't tell your story to anyone except your father and Toomey. We can trust Abe, I'm sure, but I wouldn't gamble on anybody else. Send Abe to me. Tell him to meet me at dusk tonight where the trail forks near the top of the ridge. Got any extra grub?"

"A little."

"Better let me have it. You'll last till you get home."

She did not comment on this practical but ungallant proposal. In the gloom of pre-dawn he could see that she was fumbling with the strap of her saddlebags and presently she swung closer, handing him the bags. "Anything else?" she asked.

"One thing. Have Abe bring me extra guns. I don't like to trust these Buckalew jobs."

"But what if the men are suspicious?"

"That's up to you. Put on a good act. Maybe you can start them on a quick job of ear-marking the cattle that were missed before. It might be a smart move in case the Buckalews try to make a quick raid. There's a chance that they'll get spooked up over this and want to lie low for a while. In that case they might try for a quick grab before going into hiding."

"Somehow you sound smarter today," she told him solemnly. "Maybe a few good wallops knocked some sense into your head."

"A beautiful compliment," he retorted. "And don't forget to tell pop that I'm the one who wants the ear-marking done. If I'm to pull your chestnuts out of the fire you'll have to keep building me up for the chore."

"I'd almost forgotten," she told him. "Somehow I'm not sure that the gain will be worth the trouble involved in using you."

"Sounds like we're getting ready to go around again. So I'll break it up and strike across the valley. So long. Think up some real nasty remarks for our next meeting—just so I'll know it's you."

Dawn was washing away the blackness above the Packsaddles when he crossed the creek so he put his bronc to a gallop, intent upon reaching the shelter of the foothills before full daylight could come. There might be Buckalew men in the valley by this time and he didn't want to be seen by them. From now on this could turn out to be a game of hide-and-seek and he remembered all too well the penalties for being found. He didn't want it to happen again.

He pulled up when he was well into the hills, holding his position there while he waited for full daylight. Twenty-four hours had made a big difference in his situation. Only a couple of days ago he had been faced with a puzzle. He needed to know a lot of things. Now the puzzle was gone and he knew the facts but there was scant satisfaction in the knowledge. In place of doubt was a stark reality. He was up against a gang of killers led by a malevolent old man who was just crazy enough to be especially deadly. A man couldn't afford to make any mistakes when he was facing that kind of threat.

Presently he moved on up the ridge until he found the rustler trail. Two sets of fresh prints showed, one set headed in each direction. The man who had gone up the valley to meet Soapy had evidently returned. And the rest of the gang had not made any new move.

He studied the prints with due care, remembering that a mistake would likely be fatal, then he pushed on up the trail to halt at a spot where a break in the timber gave him a chance to watch the valley below him. There he halted, resting aching bones and munching some of the saddle-grub Billy had given him. The food reminded him of her and he grinned in memory. For a spitfire she had a lot of good points.

Midafternoon brought no indication of any move on the part of the rustlers so he changed his position, heading on up the trail to the fork where Toomey was to meet him. The little man was prompt, appearing just as the sun was dropping away behind the Antelopes.

"Right on time," he told Abe. "Anything new at the ranch?"

"Nothin' that ye kin wonder about. Miss Billy told me the yarn."

"Got any idea who Soapy is?"

"Nope."

"Find anything in the upper valley?"

"Nope."

Moran grimaced at the little man's brevity. "Any message for me?"

Toomey shook his grizzled head but there was a twinkle in his eyes as he reported, "Miss Billy says fer me to keep an eye on ye. She didn't rightly send no word to ye but she says, 'Abe, don't let that idjit git into no more messes!'— so I reckon as how that's kind of a message to ye."

Johnny chuckled, partly at the idea and partly because it was such a long speech for Toomey. Then he went back to solemn matters. "What

179

about this jigger who's workin' with the rustlers? Soapy? Didn't you ever know of a Lazy J man bein' called by that handle?"

"Nope. All I kin tell ye is it ain't me—and I don't reckon it's Curly. The others I ain't knowed so long."

"Who was away from the ranch at the time when the rustler messenger met Soapy?"

"Me." The grimace and sidelong glance were almost comic. "I was still up the valley."

"Was anybody missing when you got back?"

"Nope."

Johnny decided that he had heard that word once too often. He broke off questioning and turned to the matter of taking his share of the supplies and munitions which Toomey had brought from Lazy J. Then he explained his plan.

"We're on outpost duty, Abe. We've got to know what the rustlers try to do—just as soon as they start to do it. We'll use the waiting game for a couple of days until we see if they'll make a mistake or two. If that doesn't work we'll figure out a move of our own. You set up a sentry post along the trail where you can be ready to look out over the valley in the morning. I'm going to feel my way up across the ridge until it gets too dark to move. At daybreak I want a good look at the trail in from the badlands. Don't let yourself get trapped—like I did—and if you hear any sound of movement work your way out and head for the ranch. If not, I'll try to meet you again in the mornin', likely along toward noon."

He watched thoughtfully as Abe rode down the trail in the gathering dusk. Then he picked up the reins and sent his own bronc into the climb which led across the top of the ridge. He had a hunch that his own chore was not to be an important one but he wanted to make sure, just as he had wanted to be certain about the upper valley. This rocky climb would show no trail but at the top it would be possible to read sign if any existed. Consequently he wanted to be on the spot to check it at daylight. After that he would know whether or not he could concentrate his attention on the lower trail.

He was fumbling in total darkness when he reached the top of the climb but the sound of his bronc's hoofs told him that he had passed above the rocky area. Without ceremony he picketed the animal and made cold camp beside the trail, rolling weary bones in clean blankets instead of the Buckalew soogans which had warmed him on the previous night. It made him feel a little better to be rid of the Buckalew taint even though he knew that the pain would not be out of his body for days to come. Maybe that would be a good thing. While the aches lasted he was not likely to forget that he had a real score to settle. Nor would he ignore the clear fact that his own life depended upon his efficiency in settling that score. "Stupe" Moran couldn't make any more mistakes.

The thoughts dwindled and suddenly he was staring into a graying dawn, aware that he had slept hard. Again it was painful to make himself crawl out of the bedroll but a sense of urgency helped him along. Almost two full days had passed since he had escaped from the outlaw clutches; certainly they would be making their move before long.

He munched cold grub while he stamped around along the trail, studying a considerable length of it. By the time his blood was circulating once more he knew that he had been right with his hunch. There had been no traffic over this stretch of trail since Toomey's cut-back from the scene of the dynamiting attempt. It meant that his rear would be secure and that he could focus his attention on the valley itself.

He mounted quickly and moved back down the ridge, pausing where a brook gurgled beside the steep incline. A deep drink for himself and the bronc, a splashing of cold water on a few bruises—that ended his morning's preparations for the day. Then he headed back to where he might hope to meet Abe.

Caution did not desert him. There was the chance that Toomey had slipped away during the night to make a report to the ranch, so Johnny eased into the lower trail afoot, leaving his bronc some distance up the ridge until he had assured himself that Abe had not returned. Only then did he remount and strike out to the south.

A half hour later he reached the first of the several places where the hidden trail afforded a view of the valley below. Height permitted him to see completely across the lower line of hills in mid-valley and he quickly spotted five men riding down the valley from Lazy J. Their lack of haste told him that they were probably the ranch hands setting out on the earmarking chore, so he guessed that nothing had broken at the ranch itself.

With everything looking so peaceful he decided to make another move to the south, hopeful of finding Abe at the next outlook. The little man would not have gone much farther on the previous evening and it might be possible to join up with him quickly.

The next opening in the timber proved to be closer than he had recalled and a quick look at the valley made him forget about Toomey. A rider was coming across the near half of the valley, angling up toward the lower slopes of the ridge as though intending to climb the mountain. He studied the rider closely but at the distance could not make identification. If it was another messenger, headed back toward the south after meeting Soapy, the fellow must know of still another hidden trail on the lower slopes.

Moran waited long enough to see that the five distant specks he had taken to be Lazy J men were still moving down the far side of the valley, then he sent his bronc at a run toward the next point of vantage. It might be doubly important to find Toomey now. The little man should know of this strange rider below. Meanwhile a further move to the south was putting Moran into position to get a closer look, possibly to intercept the fellow who was now working into the lower foothills.

This time he seemed to travel a long distance before the trail crossed a shoulder of rock where there was an opening to permit further study of the lower slopes. The distance made Moran uneasy about Toomey. The little man would not have come so far last evening. Why hadn't he appeared somewhere along the trail? Had he moved southward at daybreak—or had he left his post during the night? If the latter possibility were the true one . . . Moran shivered a little at the thought. Even now he might be riding headlong into the hands of the rustlers.

Still there was no sign of trouble along the hidden trail and presently he flung himself from the saddle at a spot which gave him quite an extensive view of the entire valley. The five spots identified as Lazy J riders were now working into a distant scattering of cattle and Johnny nodded his head in satisfaction. He had picked them correctly; even now they were getting at the chore of ear-marking the stock that had previously been missed. The rest of the view was not so reassuring; that extra rider was not in sight.

He held his post this time, unwilling to risk another wild ride down the trail without knowing where Abe was. The delay quickly paid off. A flicker of movement almost directly below him warned that the stranger had worked into the foothills and was traversing the shallow valleys there. Tree tops blocked off any direct view but Johnny decided that the fellow was not on any new trail but was working up the slope to strike the now familiar rustler path.

Five minutes later he caught another glimpse and knew that the guess had been correct. The stranger was still a little distance to the north, moving along a little shoulder of the mountain that would bring him to the trail at a point slightly south of Moran's position. That was enough for Johnny. He sent his bronc over the edge of the trail, taking the steep slope that led down to the shoulder. The capture of a prisoner might be worth something of a risk at this stage of the game.

The pony slid on his haunches more often than on his feet but the slope proved to be reasonably smooth and in short order Moran found himself on the narrow bench which marked the course the strange rider was taking. The side of the mountain being as it was, there was almost no other path for the fellow to take. An ambush here ought to prove effective.

He slid from the saddle, almost forgetting his aches as he knotted the bronc's reins around a dead pine and moved away some fifty feet to a clump of short trees which offered good cover. There he paused to listen and knew that he had been none too swift with his action. Already he could hear a horse coming through the tangle of underbrush.

His gun came out then and he checked its loads while he flexed the muscles of his right hand. He hoped that he would not have to shoot but he knew that he must be ready for gunfire. If this rider was like the rest of the outlaw crowd he would probably prefer a fight to a surrender. Cramps in the trigger finger couldn't be risked this morning.

The sounds came ever closer and suddenly he caught a brief glimpse of a horse and rider through the pines. He raised his gun, steadying himself as he stepped quietly into a little better position. Then he waited for his quarry to break through a screen of brush.

The six-gun was steady as the horse's head came into view, no more than fifty feet away, but then Moran grunted in disgust and let the weapon drop back to his side. After so much anticipation it was a distinct annoyance to find that the mysterious rider was Billy Whitaker. For the second time he had stalked the girl without realizing her identity.

Memory—and sight of her disheveled appearance—brought a chuckle hard on the trail of the grunt and he stepped out into the open, keeping his voice calm and casual as he asked, "What's up? Something doing at the ranch?"

She brushed back a tawny strand of hair which had come loose to dangle in her eyes, using the gesture to cover her start of surprise. He saw that she must have had quite a battle with the underbrush and branches. There was a scratch along the side of her chin, and a torn place at the shoulder of her shirt suggested hard travel. Still she managed to reply in a tone which was almost as calm as his own.

"Nothing wrong. Why do you ask?"

"Because I thought you were to keep an eye on matters at that end until I reported in from here. You're just askin' for more trouble to come blunderin' up here like this."

She flushed at his indictment. "Don't complain so much. I know what I'm doing!"

"You look it," he retorted with clear irony. "I suppose you always pick the trails that get you all ragged and torn?"

"Go ahead. Be nasty—as usual."

"Why not? You've ducked out on your chore for no good reason. Now you're in a dangerous spot. I'd think you'd have brains enough to know better."

Again she took refuge in counter-anger. "Look who's talking about brains. Even the hands are calling you 'Stupe' now."

"Who called me that?" he snapped, interest rather than irritation in his voice.

"Underhill, if that means anything. But why bother about personal matters? It would be much more intelligent to ask me why I came up here."

"Would I get an intelligent answer?"

"You would. Where is this hidden trail you told me about?"

"A little higher up the mountain. Why?"

"Lead me to it. Then we'll talk."

"Come along—but I'm surprised that a girl who's rated the best tracker in the valley didn't find it from the other end."

"I didn't look," she snapped. "You said that the trail went to the top of the ridge and then came down again. I wanted to take a short-cut to this part of it."

"Sounds like you. Always the hard way." He went back to his bronc, mounted, and sent the animal up the side of the ridge. The girl followed close behind, neither of them offering any further comment until they were side by side on the rustler trail.

Chapter Thirteen

JOHNNY MORAN was purposely severe as he faced the girl. Her presence on the mountain added considerably to the risks of the situation. "Better make it good," he warned. "I don't like the idea of having you around if the Buckalews move in on us."

"Don't bother to qualify your remarks; you just don't like me around." She turned her back on him and began to survey the valley which was now completely in view. For a moment or two Johnny thought she was simply being stubborn but then he realized that she was studying the distant forms of the Lazy J men.

"Looks like they're ear-markin'," he commented. "You got that part done all right, I reckon, before you started to kick over the traces."

She let out a little exclamation of disappointment as she turned back to face him again. If she had even heard his sarcasm she didn't pay attention. Instead she gave him a look of some embarrassment as she murmured, "I think I made a mistake."

"Which one?"

She motioned toward the valley. "They're not working alone out there."

He didn't understand for a moment and she explained, her tone indicating that the words were coming with an effort. "I thought I saw a chance to get a line on the traitor in our crew. I assumed that each man would do the ear-marking work alone, so I came up here to spy on them, figuring that I could spot the disloyal hand by watching to see which one was skipping a suspicious number of cows."

Moran showed her no mercy. "Kinda stupid for a gal who claims to know the cattle business so doggone well. It would take a mighty good man to ear-mark full-sized steers alone. One jigger might handle a calf but he won't handle real beef alone—if he's got good sense. I'm kinda astonished that you figured your pappy's old-timers would try it."

"Go ahead," she grumbled. "Rub it in. I was dumb."

"Dumber'n you think," he agreed. "You didn't need to make any flyin' trip up here to spot Soapy."

"Why not? Do you know who he is?"

"I do now. You just told me a few minutes ago."

"But how could . . . ?"

"Think a bit. What was the last time any of the Lazy J men went to Dragoon Bend?"

She looked surprised at the question but answered readily enough. "I think Curly was last.

About two months ago. My father and I usually run the errands."

"Who did you tell about my reputation at Sawmill Springs?"

"Nobody. I'm saving that—remember?"

"Then no one at Lazy J should know that I was ever called 'Stupe' Moran. Right?"

"Right unless they heard it a long time ago."

"Nobody ever called me that until about two months back. So the man who called me 'Stupe' to you last night must have got the word from somebody on the outside. And . . ."

"And only the traitor has been hearing from outside. I think you're absolutely right!"

"Thanks. So it's Underhill, the man you thought was the only good hand on the payroll."

She grimaced. "Do you have to remind me of every little error I make?"

"I don't have to—but it's kinda fun. You didn't haul in your slack none when you was rawhidin' me on the same score."

The grimace of exasperation turned into a wry grin which made her seem almost like an urchin who had been caught stealing apples. "Johnny Moran," she laughed. "I ought to punch you right in the nose."

His own smile was a signal of surrender. "Don't. It's too sore now."

It brought another change of expression and

she became instantly solicitous. "Are you feeling all right—with all those bumps?"

"I'll live—if the Buckalews don't get hold of me again. But don't get on to that subject. You high-tail it right back for the ranch. I've got to mosey on down this trail and pick up Toomey. He oughta be comin' back by this time."

"Where is he?"

"I don't know. He oughta be a little piece to the south."

"Then I'll go with you. You might learn something that I can take back with me."

He started to protest but she waved the objection aside. "Don't always be starting arguments. You know it makes more sense to handle it this way."

He shrugged. "All right. Come along—but if anything starts to bust loose you git out in a hurry. Right back along this trail and across the valley. Understand?"

"Yes, Mister Moran," she said meekly.

Less than a mile down the trail Billy broke the somewhat grim silence to point at the ground. "Wait a minute. We're riding over fresh sign."

Moran pulled up sharply, aware that he had been careless again. He had been assuming that Toomey was ahead, serving as sentry against an outlaw move. It was not a safe assumption and the girl's words gave him something of a start.

He was looking at the ground even as he pulled the bronc to a halt, seeing fresh hoofprints in the patches of soft dirt. Surprisingly they were the marks of a horse being driven hard down the trail to the south. Evidently Abe had been striking out for the southern part of the valley—and in a big hurry.

Moran wondered what it meant. Could it be that he had misjudged Abe? Had the little man been the traitor, after all? He forced the conclusion from his mind and swung to watch Billy as she dismounted and ran back along the narrow trail. It reminded him that the Lazy J hands had rated her as a first-class tracker. Seeing her now in action he decided that she knew what she was about.

He tied his own pony to a branch and slid from the saddle to follow her. The sign was clear enough. The horseman had just been getting up speed here, the bronc's shoes digging in as his strides lengthened.

"He came out of here," Billy announced, pointing to a clump of pines which flanked the trail at the spot where the ground leveled off a little. She was moving into the timber as she spoke, bending close to study the sign. Moran followed silently, watching the brisk way she cast about to pick up every mark. They found a spot where a man had slept but Johnny could not quite piece out the full story until Billy began to explain it aloud, excitement ringing clear in her voice.

"It was Abe, all right," she said positively. "He must have stopped here after dark. When he woke up this morning he wandered across the trail to a spot where he could get a peek at the valley. When he came back he was at the dead run. After that it's all hurry. I'd say he saw something pretty important."

Johnny nodded with a frown on his face. The girl's reconstruction was sound, he thought, but he couldn't figure Abe moving out to the south. The order had been just the opposite. "Wonder why he went that way?" he mused. "I told him to get back with a quick report if he saw anything."

"Maybe this was something that couldn't wait."

Moran started for his horse. "Then we'll find out what it was. There's nothing out of the way in the valley now. You strike out for the ranch and tell 'em what we've seen. I'll try to catch Abe. If he struck out in such a hurry I'd better get on his trail pronto."

She reached her horse first, vaulting into the saddle before he could offer a helping hand. "How far is it to the end of this trail?" she asked.

"Two-three miles, maybe. Why?"

"I'm going with you. Then I'll have a chance to know more—and it will be easier to get help if you need it. The sign says there's nothing to worry about on this trail and I'll be closer to our men in the valley if I go this way instead of back along the ridge."

He grinned briefly at the way she had poured out the volley of argument. "You win," he agreed. "But don't try to keep pace with me. You've got to save your bronc for emergencies and I reckon this hammer-head can take it."

"Right," she agreed. "Hit it up."

He was a bit annoyed to find that he could not shake her off. She was mounted on the same wiry little buckskin he had seen that day at the creek and the animal was much fresher than his own mount. There was little space between them when they broke out of the open country at the south end of Lazy J range.

There Moran slowed the pace, studying the trail which he had been seeing but briefly as he galloped. Abe's bronc had still been hitting a fast clip at this point.

"What do you make of it?" Billy called, eyes alight with excitement.

"Nothing—yet. Ought to know mighty soon. There'll be sign that'll tell me what prodded Toomey into so much action. You swing off there to the right; you'll be able to pick up the crew within six to eight miles."

"Not just yet, mister. I'll stick with you till we know something. I can't go to the boys and just look excited. They'll want to know what's up— and what Abe was doing."

Moran did not argue. After having seen the girl demonstrate her ability as a tracker he was willing to have her along. Already he had begun to visualize the situation as it must have shaped up, but he wanted her to confirm the guess that was in his mind.

The confirmation was not long in coming. They had splashed through the shallow waters of Antelope Creek and were still following Toomey's sign when they found what Moran had anticipated. Four riders had hazed thirty-odd head of stock past this point only hours before. They had been headed down the valley at a remarkably fast pace.

"It adds up," he said tersely. "They came up the creek durin' the night. Likely had their stock already spotted. Maybe it was some of the same bunch they missed on last week when your father busted in on 'em. Anyway they shoved the beef out durin' the night and Abe woke up just in time to see the herd movin' outa sight. He knew it was too late to ask for help so he started to trail 'em alone. Nervy old cuss, ain't he?"

She nodded soberly. "I think you're right." It was quite an admission, considering their past record for disagreements but it was no more unusual than her ensuing question. "What can we do about it?" Neither of them seemed to notice the change.

"You get the boys," Moran told her. "I'll follow

Abe and hope I can be in time to side him if he gets into trouble."

"What about Underhill?"

"Talk to Curly—or Glaspey—on the quiet. Try to keep any of the others from even guessing that you know anything. Let Curly get the drop on Underhill and tie him up. Then send the crew to trail Abe and me. You can take Underhill to the ranch as a prisoner—but make sure that he's tied up plenty tight before you start out with him."

She nodded briskly, all tendency to argue forgotten. "Right," she said. Then she was spurring the buckskin hard up the bank of Antelope Creek.

Moran permitted himself an appreciative glance but then he turned to the task at hand. It was now a little past noon and the rustlers must have been in this part of the valley shortly after daybreak. That gave them a start of perhaps six hours. Even allowing for their haste they would not have been able to push cows too fast. Toomey must be following hard on their heels already. With a little luck this could turn out to be the break Moran had hoped for.

Maybe it was even better than he had hoped. The cattle had been picked up during the night and the thieves would not have been able to pick out stock as they previously had done. In the darkness they would have taken ear-marked steers along with the others. This time there would be evidence against them.

That was the bright side, at any rate. Catching the bandits with that evidence was another matter. The very fact that the raid had been staged indicated that the rustlers had been willing to adopt desperation measures. Either they wanted to attempt one last haul before going into hiding or they were deliberately bidding for a showdown. Moran thought it to be the latter. Their plan to hang him as a warning suggested boldness and he had a feeling that this raid had been planned to bring on a climax.

Presently the trail began to work across the open part of the valley toward the Antelopes. That fitted with what he had learned while prisoner. The gang had a hideout beyond the hills, a valley where they held their stolen beef until ready to make shipment.

By the time he sighted McSorley's place he decided that a talk with the old rancher might be worth the few minutes' delay that it would cost. Cutting away from the traces of the cattle drive he headed directly for Pigpen, quickly becoming aware that the lanky oldster was watching him from a corner of the corral. The man did not seem to be armed but Johnny remembered his caution. McSorley was now a known enemy and might be inclined to play it the tough way. Better to make sure that the six-gun was loose in its holster than to discover too late that it was going to stick at a crucial moment.

He grinned a little at his own thoughts. It was not a happy grin. Back of it was the memory of what had happened to him when last he had taken too much for granted. There were plenty of aches as reminders. He didn't dare permit it to happen again.

McSorley's lean old face was haggard and drawn as he came out to meet Moran. It was obvious that he realized his own sorry plight but it was not clear how he proposed to act in the emergency. Johnny came on quietly but his gun hand was tense and ready. McSorley was desperate and desperate men sometimes do foolish things.

"How long since the rustlers passed here?" he asked abruptly.

McSorley didn't dodge either the question or the implication that went with it. "Four-five hours," he said miserably.

"How many of 'em?"

"Four. The two Buckalew boys, Squint Oldroyd and Red Farrell. They had mebbe thirty head."

Moran nodded with some relief. McSorley was ready to open up. "When did Abe Toomey go by?"

"Almost in their dust. He was doggin' 'em hard but I don't figger they'd spotted him yet."

"Did he talk to you?"

"Nope."

"Know where they're headed?"

McSorley's tired eyes opened as he stared straight at Moran. "Look, feller. I been a dam' fool but I ain't in the gang. I dunno how they run things and I ain't clear on where they take their stock. All I done was . . ."

"All you did was keep your mouth shut because you were afraid of Buckalew and what he could say about you. Right?"

"That's about the size of it. He had . . ."

"I know. You figured he'd get you in trouble over that old shootin' scrape. You were a damn fool, all right. In the first place they wouldn't arrest you again for the same shootin'. In the second place Buckalew could not open his mouth without making himself an open target for a perjury charge. And in the third place it wasn't any secret in the first place. Plenty of people knew about it and didn't hold it against you. You've been throwing down your friends for nothing."

The old rancher's jaw had dropped at each statement until he looked almost comic with his mouth so far open. Then the jaw snapped shut and he seemed to reach a decision. "Yuh mean Rance Whitaker knew about me?"

"He didn't know you were watching rustlers steal his cattle."

McSorley didn't seem to realize that his real question had gone unanswered. The grim look came back to his wrinkled countenance and he started to turn away. "Wait fer me while I git me a gun," he snapped.

"Hold it," Moran interrupted. "You wait here for the Lazy J boys. They don't know about you so they won't ask questions. Bring 'em along pronto while I shove ahead and catch Abe. He's likely to get himself into trouble and need some help."

Suddenly McSorley turned. "One thing yuh better know," he cautioned. "Ed Underhill's part of the gang."

"We already know it," Moran told him, wheeling his horse to head back toward the trail of the stolen stock. "But it's a point to keep in mind. Look out for yourself."

Then he was gone, spurring the tiring horse as he tried to make up the minutes he had lost at Pigpen. He could only hope that Abe Toomey had not let his enthusiasm run away with him.

Chapter Fourteen

T HE TRAIL of the stolen beef was easy to follow and within the hour Moran found himself among the low hills which marked the end of the Antelope chain. It was in this region that he had camped and been surprised by the Buckalews. The memory was warning enough, even without the sore places to accent it. He was approaching the rustler hideout and the danger would be increasing with every yard of distance.

Still he found time to study the sign, marveling at the way the beef had been hustled along. Those riders had been relentless, driving the cattle in what must have been a virtual stampede all the way. Evidently the herders had not paused to make any passes at the man who had tailed them across the valley. Since it seemed certain that they must have noticed Toomey it was significant that they had elected to ignore him. Moran didn't like the implications in that idea. Either the outlaws didn't fear a man who was so far from any assistance—or they were deliberately leading him into a trap where they might dispose of him at their leisure. Johnny guessed that it was the latter.

The afternoon was more than half gone when

he saw dust ahead, just beyond a fringe of hills which broke away from the rest of the tumbled chain. That would be the stolen beef. He was finally overtaking them in spite of the speed with which they had been driven.

"Looks like it might be the edge of the hill country," he said aloud, trying to square his present observations with what he had already noticed about the mountain spur. "Sorry I didn't get a chance to look things over a mite before the Buckalews put a loop on me. It might come in real handy to know the layout o' that hole o' theirs."

His regrets were strengthened, only some ten minutes later. Just as he sent the tired bronc into the ascent of the hill chain he caught the distant spatter of gunshots. The trap must have sprung on Abe Toomey. Now Johnny Moran had to ride headlong into country which he had never seen, country which was probably well suited to the ambush which the outlaws had just sprung on Abe.

Still there was no hesitation. He dug spurs into the weary bronc, dimly aware of his own regret at having to use the animal so roughly. The big roan had done noble duty during the past few days and it was a marvel that it still had the stamina to respond at all. They went up across the shoulder of a ridge with the gunshots still sounding angrily ahead of them as though to lend urgency to the occasion.

The trail wound through timber at the crest of the climb and then—with a suddenness that was startling—they were in the open, the declining sun filling the sky ahead with a hot glare. This was the last line of hills before the mountain spur flattened out into desert country. The rustler hideout would have to be close now since it would be concealed by hills. The showdown was at hand—and Johnny would have to make his attack with the sun in his eyes. He could not afford the luxury of a roundabout attack if he hoped to be any good to Abe Toomey.

He still could not see anything except the timber directly ahead of him but he knew that Abe was still holding out. Twice he had heard additional bursts of firing, each time followed by a succession of well-spaced shots. The pattern was repeated now as he began to ease down from the summit of the ridge. Abe was still defending himself with some skill.

He tried to take hope from the thought, but his mind warned him that there was scant room for optimism. The rustlers would not have lured Abe so close to their hideout if they had not felt pretty certain of killing him to keep him from disclosing their secret. Abe was in a tight spot—and Johnny Moran had to stick his neck into the same dangerous noose in order to help the little man.

He permitted the tired horse to slow down

as they worked around the end of a peculiarly-shaped rocky ledge. The shots rang out in a fresh burst, serving to keep him apprised of his own position in relation to the gunfight. He was only a few hundred yards away now but the terrain was such that he still could not see any part of the battleground. The shooting was slightly below him, he thought, but the trail was pretty much on the level now. It meant that he had to be prepared for some abrupt change in the character of the trail so he let the bronc take it easy for a minute or two. Blundering into a sharp drop at high speed would be almost as foolish as exposing himself heedlessly before locating Abe's position.

Suddenly he thought about Billy Whitaker. Would she be able to bring help in time? A quick calculation was not reassuring. The Lazy J riders would be hours behind him at the start and they would not have hit the sort of pace he had maintained. This would have to be a two-man battle. Toomey and Moran were on their own.

Then the trail began to pitch downward and he could catch glimpses of the country beyond. Part of the picture suggested itself when he saw the tops of a line of low, stony hills beyond and below. On this side of the mountains the ground did not level off as gradually as it did to the southeast. Here a series of ridges broke the slope, the low spots between the ridges forming deep pockets that were almost gorges. It was from one of these holes that the firing was coming. This would be the hole which had served as headquarters for the rustlers, the spot where they concealed stolen cattle until brands had been blotted. Today it had been the spot for the springing of a trap on Abe Toomey.

Moran fingered his six-gun tentatively but pulled the hand away to reach forward and draw the Winchester from its boot. The longer range weapon seemed like the better choice. He pulled up where a few lonely pines clung desperately to the loose soil between the rocks, picketing the weary bronc in the most sheltered spot available. Then he went forward afoot, aiming for a break in the slope which he hoped would give him a view of the lower slopes. A single gunshot sounded from the near distance so he knew that he was hard upon the scene of action.

A dozen strides put him in position to grasp the situation more completely. Directly ahead the ground sloped away so sharply that the cattle trail went down at a long angle into a rocky pocket that was almost completely shut in by rock-strewn ridges. He knew at a glance that this was the place he had been thinking about, the place the rustlers had mentioned when he was their prisoner. He could see cattle milling around far below him but he could not see a human being anywhere.

The flat silence could mean but one thing. Abe

was still putting up a fight, keeping the outlaws discreetly under cover. Otherwise they would be showing themselves. No shot had been heard since Johnny had left his bronc but the last one had sounded mighty close, too close for hasty moves. Maybe Abe had fired it and maybe he hadn't. Johnny could only guess that he was approaching the skirmish from the right side.

He shaded his eyes against the glare of approaching sunset, watching for a movement which might offer either a target or information. For several long, tense minutes he had no luck at all but, then, he caught a flicker of motion some sixty yards to his right. He had seen it only out of the corner of his eye but he knew that a man had jumped hastily across an open space along the top of the slope.

For an instant Johnny thought it must have been Abe but then he realized his error. If Abe had been up here on the high ground he wouldn't have been acting like that. The little man would be trying to get away with the vital information he had gained.

The thought suggested a better explanation. The rustlers had spotted Toomey on their back trail and had planned their ambush carefully. When they sent the stolen beef down the slanting trail into the pocket they had left a man on the high ground behind them. It had been a good trap but somehow it had not quite succeeded. Abe was forted up down there on the slope, holding off the other outlaws and trying to keep from being picked off by the man who had closed the trap on him.

Moran grinned thinly as he swung the Winchester. Apparently the sniper did not yet know that help had arrived for Toomey. Pretty soon the fellow would shift his position again as he tried to get a vantage point for killing Abe. When he did . . . Moran grinned again, remembering the treatment he had received at the hands of the outlaws. It would be a real pleasure to cut the odds down a bit.

For what seemed like hours he studied the terrain over the Winchester's sights. He saw that the ground was mostly rocks or rocky ledges affording the hidden enemy considerable protection. At the same time he guessed that Abe must be in a position to cover the area with gunfire or the rustler would not be resorting to so much careful maneuvering. It made him feel a little more hopeful about Toomey's position but he didn't permit himself to get curious. Abe could wait; the important matter now was to watch for that man among the rocks to make a new move.

It was a shrill yell from below that broke the tense silence. For an instant Moran wondered what had gone wrong down there but then he knew that the yell had been a signal. From several points in the basin gunfire began to rattle and he had a quick intuition about its meaning. The other outlaws were trying to take Abe's attention while the man at the head of the slope moved to a better sniping post. Johnny tensed himself, easing the hammer back until it clicked softly.

Suddenly the outlaw popped up, scrambling straight toward Johnny. There was a brief instant when his head came into view, a moment in which Moran saw a narrow, dark face with close-set eyes and a snarling mouth. It was one of the Buckalew sons. He wasn't sure which but he had a feeling that it was not the one who had tried to trap Billy Whitaker.

Johnny squeezed the trigger even as the thought raced through his mind. Maybe it wasn't sporting to shoot a man this way, but a fellow didn't have much choice when he was dealing with this kind of people. It was kill or be killed—and he had to save Abe Toomey.

The Winchester bucked once and Moran jacked in a fresh cartridge, holding the weapon ready while he stared grimly down the barrel. There was no need to fire again. The outlaw had plunged forward on his face, his weapon clattering into view between a couple of rocks. Moran studied the situation for a long minute, then drew in a deep breath. It was not a pleasant feeling to have killed even an outlaw in that manner, but the inhalation brought a quick ache to his ribs and the pain drove all qualms away.

"Tally one," he said aloud. "That squares me for some of those kicks in the brisket. Next, I'll get even for this lop-sided jaw."

He knew that he was talking to make himself feel better, so he broke off abruptly, listening to the shouts from below. Evidently the other rustlers had witnessed the death of Buckalew. A chunk of lead whined angrily against the rock above Moran's head and he glanced upward, trying to estimate the course of the bullet from the mark it had left. The shot had certainly come from below, not from some spot along the ledge itself.

He crouched low, inching forward to peer down the slope in an effort to locate the man who had fired. He was in time to see a head drop back out of sight behind a boulder so he held his position, shoving the Winchester out until he could aim at the spot. Perhaps he could score again before the enemy could know what was happening to them.

This time the luck did not hold. The fellow behind the boulder played it safe, keeping discreetly out of sight, and after a lengthy interval Moran's patience wore out. Further surprise seemed hopeless; it would be better to locate Abe and let the little man know the facts.

"You down there, Abe?" he called.

"Who wants to know?" The reply was cautious and a little querulous.

"Moran. How are you makin' out?"

This time he knew that the reply came from a little distance below and to the left. "I'm holed up in the rocks. They got my bronc."

"You hit?"

"Nope."

Moran chuckled. Toomey's conversation was reaching its regular level. "Any chance o' gettin' back here?"

"Nope. I'm kinda sewed up."

"How many of 'em down there?"

"Three—four, I reckon. Did yuh git the varmint up there on top?"

"I got him."

"Good. He was makin' a dam' pest o' hisself." There was a pause and then the little man added reluctantly, as though pained at the necessity of having to talk so much, "Keep an eye on the critter about a quarter way down the grade. I kin keep the rest behavin' theirselves."

A rattle of shots came to dispute this boast and Toomey's gun boomed a reply. At his shot the man behind the boulder showed a shoulder and Moran drove him to cover with a fast slug that either missed him or just nicked him. Johnny couldn't tell which. Then the silence came down once more.

The sun was lying right on the crest of the lower hill chain now and Moran found it hard to stare into the area where the enemy lay. Abe's voice came again. "Got help, Moran?"

"Sure," Johnny lied quickly, aware that the enemy could hear him. "The other boys will show when we need 'em."

"Tell 'em to make it soon. I just got me a furrow in the neck. It's bleedin' some. Not serious, though."

"Take care of it. I'll keep 'em from rushin' you."

"Fair enough."

"Have you got the others spotted? I'm already taking good care of the gent behind the boulder."

"Keep watchin' him. He's ornery. The others are below the ledge where the trail pitches down. That's how they dang near got me. I busted out into sight and they was layin' fer me. They got the bronc on the fust fire but I was lucky enough to fall behind him."

Moran shifted his position, inching forward until he had a better view of the rough slope. He could see the slanting strata of outcropping which served as a pathway to the lower parts of the freak valley but he could see no movement along it. The men who were using it as a rocky bastion were keeping themselves carefully out of sight.

There was a long interval of silent waiting, Moran uneasily aware that he was squinting hard in his effort to avoid the rays of that slowly setting sun. While it was in its present position he must be showing very plainly to anyone looking up the slope. In order to keep himself from being a first-class target he had to keep those heads down so they couldn't look.

Suddenly he caught a flicker of movement out of the tail of his eye. The man behind the nearer boulder was trying something. The Winchester swung to cover the spot but instantly a new move showed on the lower slope. Evidently the rustlers down there had been watching without being able to risk bringing a gun to bear. Now they were trying to catch him in the interval while he was covering the other fellow.

He flattened himself hard against the rocks as he snapped the rifle back to the left. A shoulder and a hand had come up beside a head. Johnny didn't try to aim. He simply slammed a bullet in the right general direction, having the satisfaction of seeing the head disappear. That was the important thing; he had to keep them down until the coming of darkness would permit Toomey to slip away.

He could hear them talking among themselves down there but he could not make out what they were saying. It occurred to him that once more he was waiting for sunset, just as he had done that night in the badlands. This time, however, darkness would offer complications. The rustlers might attempt to close in or they might elect to slip away under cover of night. Neither alternative was to Moran's liking. A close-up fight in the darkness would be pretty nasty; and he didn't care to think of the gang getting away now. This was the chance to close out the account and he wanted to make it good. He didn't want to let anyone have the opportunity to say that Johnny Moran had blundered again.

A little mental calculation was not too cheering. The other Lazy J riders must have been a full hour behind him when Billy reached them and it wasn't at all likely that they had improved on that interval. Their cow ponies would have been tired from the work of ear-marking, in no condition for the sort of ride ahead of them. Probably they would have light enough to follow the trail well into the hills, but Johnny didn't think they would be able to reach the scene of the fight before full darkness could come down. And if they came up in the night there would be the risk of hasty shooting with himself and Abe Toomey caught in the middle.

The sun slipped out of sight while he thought about it but the encroaching shadows did not seem to encourage the outlaws. Evidently they too were waiting for night. Moran wished that he knew why. He didn't have any idea whether to prepare for a chase or a defense of his present position.

Then Abe's voice came up out of the shadows. "Gettin' dark, Moran. Why don't yo' and the other boys stir 'em up a mite?"

The answer came jeeringly from behind the boulder. "Because there ain't no other boys, that's why! He's bluffin', Toomey. But we ain't."

Moran didn't like the sound of that even though it answered his question. The rustlers were not planning to retreat. They were on familiar ground and they were clearly planning to overwhelm their annoyers as soon as they felt that the advantage was on their side. Johnny decided that it was the smart way for them to handle it. Probably they didn't believe that any word had been sent back to Lazy J. Consequently they might easily hide their trail by killing off the only man who knew the facts. From their point-of-view—and with their limited knowledge of the facts—it seemed like a better bet than a harried retreat.

He kept his voice calm as he called out, "Who's your friend, Abe? He seems to know you—even if he ain't what you might call smart."

"Dunno his name," Toomey yelled back. "He's a ugly redhead. I seen that much."

Johnny recalled the names McSorley had given him. "Must be Red Farrell," he announced cheerfully. "They say he's right ugly. Wanted as a horse thief, among other things."

"Listen to Stupe!" the raucous voice shouted. "Gittin' smart now that it's too late. Yuh're my own personal meat, Moran. Yuh killed a pard o' mine over there at the old hideout. I'm claimin' yuh fer that."

215

"Come on out and stake your claim," Johnny replied.

"Yaah! Don't figger I'm that dumb jest because yo' are. I'll git yuh in my own way."

"Wanta bet?"

"I would—but I can't collect from a dead man."

The exchange of grisly humor ended as a gun boomed, its report sounding deep and hollow on the still air of dusk. Instantly two other weapons barked in reply and Moran drove a slug at one of the flashes below him. It was Abe's voice that rang out in explanation. "Yuh almost talked the polecat into showin' hisself, Moran. I ain't so sure but what I winged him at that."

The man behind the boulder hooted in derision. "Stop dreamin', Abe. Yuh wasn't even close."

Moran broke in, studying the creeping shadows every minute. "How's the neck, Abe?"

"Good enough."

"Get the blood stopped?"

"I reckon so."

Again the grim humorist behind the rock offered a comment. "We'll soon git it started again, Abe. Why don't yuh jest go ahead and bleed to death in comfort?"

This time it was Moran who shattered the flow of deadly comedy. A dark spot had moved below the long ledge and he tried to center his sights on it. In the darkness he could not be sure of his front sight but his shot brought a quick

216

curse down there. Again he could hear shouted remarks but the distance was too great for him to distinguish the words. He could only guess that he had scored a hit and that the outlaws were talking about it.

The blackness came down rapidly after that and Moran kept silent. He was expecting Abe to start moving at any moment now and he didn't want to draw a reply which might indicate to the enemy that Toomey was out in the open. For the present it was enough to strain his eyes into the gloom, hopeful of seeing something that would serve as a target. At the same time he was keeping an ear cocked for sounds in the rear which might indicate the arrival of help. That was one reason why he had been willing to try that almost futile shot at the man down the hill. The gunshot might help to guide the Lazy J riders to him.

Chapter Fifteen

THE waiting began to make him jittery. In his eagerness to catch up with the rustlers he had given no thought to personal danger but now he was reminded of that other dusk when vicious bullets had hunted him out. Tonight might turn out to be a replica of the fight in the hidden valley across the Packsaddles. It was certain that the men down there in the gloom would try to make it something of the sort—but with a different ending. He had earned both their hatred and their fear; tonight they would try to pay off a score and at the same time eliminate him as a threat. Having had one sample of the sort of treatment they handed out he had no illusions.

It required an effort for him to stifle the urge for frenzied action. It would have been easier to make some sort of move instead of lying there in silence but he knew that his game had to be the passive one no matter how much it irked him. None of the old Johnny Moran wildness now. He had to wait and listen, forcing himself to restrain the almost frantic desire for a movement that would relieve some of the nervous tension.

Oddly, he wondered about old Buckalew. The gang leader ought to be down there with the others but his snarling voice had not yet been heard. It was a wonder that the old maniac hadn't driven his men into a headlong charge after the death of his son. It made Moran a bit uneasy to think about it. There was no telling what a fanatic like old Buckalew would do—but it probably would be vicious and desperate.

The silence continued until nightfall really became complete. Then little sounds began to drift up to Moran out of the swiftly blackening pocket and he scanned the gloom with dogged interest. Several men were already moving around down there but he could not make out even a moving shadow. He guessed that some of the sound meant a move on the part of Abe Toomey so he knew that he would not dare to fire even if he could spot a target. There was the real risk that he might fire at Abe. Nor did he venture to do any talking because it might call the enemy's attention to whatever move Toomey might be trying.

Straining his ears to interpret each tiny sound, he knew again the pain of having to wait and do nothing. He could not relax even though he did not dare risk action. The thought bothered him so much that he found himself gripping the Winchester with fingers that pained from the strain. Fighting wasn't half as bad as this waiting game.

Partly to relieve the tension and partly because

219

it needed doing he slipped fresh shells into the magazine of the rifle. He had not been forgetting, he told himself a little wryly; it was simply that he had not found the chance to reload. Until the last few minutes he had not ventured to take his eyes from the scene of action long enough to shove in new cartridges.

He smiled crookedly in the gloom as he let the thought drift through his mind. Would Billy Whitaker have believed it if she had been here? Or would she have accused him of his notorious carelessness? Probably it would have been the latter. He seemed to get into a fight with her on every possible occasion—with or without a reasonable excuse.

Thinking back over those tiffs he concluded that he hadn't been half as much annoyed at her as he had pretended. He just hoped he could live through the present emergency so as to work up another wrangle over something unimportant.

The soft scuffling sounds persisted but he was more relaxed now. There was no point in holding the weapon so tightly when he didn't dare fire a shot anyway. Lowering the weapon he raised himself on his elbows, listening intently as he tried to guess what was happening in front and below.

Suddenly he located one of the sounds, close at hand and a bit to the left. He swung the Winchester until it covered a shadow which he thought had moved. Then he whispered, "Abe. Is that you?"

Toomey's hoarse wheeze floated to his ears in reply. "Git ready to gimme a hand," the man gasped. "I'm kinda tuckered out."

Johnny lowered the rifle silently to the ground and inched forward as Abe came up over the edge of the slope. One groping hand caught Toomey's lean wrist and Moran could sense that the man was almost at the point of collapse.

"Easy," Toomey whispered. "I'm bleedin' again."

Johnny caught hold under the armpits, dragging his partner back to a protected position. Then he fumbled at the sodden mass of cloth which had been tied at Abe's neck. "Been bleeding long?" he asked. "This is sticky in places but dried hard in others."

"I stopped it once, I reckon, but it busted out again when I started to crawl up the rocks."

Moran used his own neckerchief to hold Abe's crude dressing in place. "Sing out if I pull this too tight," he cautioned. "Can't afford to strangle you just to stop a bit o' blood." He tried to make it sound easy but he knew from the feel that Toomey had bled badly. The man's shirt was sticky all down one side.

When the job was done as well as conditions would permit he gave Abe a pat on the other shoulder. "Lie flat and don't move. You're out of

221

the line of fire now so I'll try to prod the boys into a bit of action. It'll confuse them and give us time to let that blood clot again. Likewise it ought to give our men a lead so they'll know where we are."

"When do yuh figger they'll reach us?"

"Hard to tell. I guessed they'd be about two hours behind us. That makes 'em overdue already. But forget it. Just keep quiet and let me play some games with our little chums down the slope."

He crawled back to his rifle but did not pick it up. Instead he backed up about a yard and gathered several cobbles of fair size. One of these he threw hard in the direction of the boulder which had sheltered the red-headed outlaw, the other was lobbed more easily to the left. The resulting clatter was pleasingly noisy and Moran let out a sudden shout. "Is that you, Abe?"

The ruse brought fast results. Gunfire boomed from several points on the slope, bullets whining angrily into the night over Moran's head. He chuckled to himself and kept down. The gunmen below were raking the exposed slope in an effort to score a blind hit on the man they thought was scrambling for cover.

Johnny waited until the fire died down, then pushed himself forward a little and tossed another rock far to the left. This time he didn't want slugs drawn toward himself. Lifting the Winchester into position he spotted the orange jets as a rustler fired at the new noise. Two fast shots by Johnny brought a howl of pain and then he was down again, letting the enemy send a new volley over his head. So far the game was working out rather satisfactorily.

"That'll slow 'em up a bit," he muttered to Abe. "Let 'em waste their ammunition."

"Wonder what's keepin' our crew?" Toomey asked weakly.

"Hard to tell. Maybe I just figured wrong." He explained swiftly the events of the day, telling Abe how he had come to estimate the time it would require for help to arrive.

"Sounds right," Toomey murmured. "Somethin' musta gone sour. Do yuh reckon McSorley mighta put up a fight?"

"More likely they've had trouble with Underhill. He could have been a bit suspicious."

"I reckon he was," Abe said shortly. He had not commented when Moran told him of the reason for picking Underhill as the traitor, but he seemed to accept it.

"Better not talk any more," Moran whispered. "Try to get back a bit of strength. If those rascals flank us we'll have to move."

Toomey grunted and Johnny went back toward the brink to throw more rocks. This time he didn't get any bites. The fish were getting smart. He listened for some minutes but could hear nothing except the diminishing clatter of a cobble which had continued to roll on down the slope. Evidently the rustlers were going to play his own game with him; they were going to keep silent and wait for a move.

Or were they? Maybe they knew another way to reach the rim of the valley. Maybe they were already scaling the slope to make a flank attack. If so they would have a certain advantage. Moran would not be able to fire at anyone coming up from the rear because he would be fearful of hitting his own reinforcements. It was not a happy thought but for the moment he didn't know what he could do about it. Retreat was practically out of the question with but one horse available and Toomey in such a serious condition.

Chapter Sixteen

THE night did not seem quite so dark when Moran looked out across the void. In the bright starlight he could make out the far rim of the pocket and the sight started him to thinking about the geography of his position. There had been neither time nor opportunity for him to make a study of the place but he knew that he must be exposed on either side. Thus far he had been in a good position because every enemy was on low ground in front of him, but they certainly would not stay there. Even now they were probably scaling the slope at some distant point, preparing to close in along the ledge or from behind the cover of the low crags.

He tried another rock but again there was only an answering clatter as the stone rattled down into the valley. Crawling on hands and knees he went back to Abe. "Don't move, Abe," he cautioned. "But tell me what happened to your rifle. We may need all the guns we can muster before long."

"Under my hoss," Toomey breathed. "The critter fell on it. I couldn't git it loose."

Moran considered for a moment. There was a chance that he might recover the weapon but the odds were against him. He didn't know exactly where Abe had gone down and it wasn't an easy place to search for in the darkness. And even if he found it there might be nothing to gain. The weapon might be pinned down or broken. "Stay quiet," he cautioned again. "I'm goin' out along the ledge to the right. Even if you hear somebody movin' around you'll be safer to keep a dead silence. That way if I hear somebody move I'll know it ain't you."

"Where yuh goin'?" Abe wanted to know.

"After Buckalew's gun. It might come in handy."

He worked his way cautiously along the top of the slant, trying to avoid loose rocks. It seemed likely that one or more of his enemies might be out there ahead of him and he wanted to have a chance of hearing them first.

It was slow work, all the more tedious because he had nothing to guide him. Trying to judge his course, estimate distance, and listen for enemies all at the same time kept him pretty busy. Twice he almost slipped over the edge of the rocks and finally he began to wonder if he had not gone too far. It seemed as though he had crawled a quarter of a mile, at least, while the dead outlaw had been less than a hundred yards away.

Once he heard a suspicious sound back toward the hills but it did not occur again and he decided that he had heard the stamping of his own bronc back there in the gulch. A coyote yelped in the distance while somewhere nearer at hand a night bird's cry broke the stillness of the crags. It was getting a bit eerie but there was nothing to do but go on with the chore at hand.

Then he put his hand against something that was certainly cloth. It gave him a start that almost hurt but he braced himself to reach out again. This time he knew that he was touching the dead body of young Buckalew. One of the rustler's arms was stretched out ahead of him, just as he had fallen, and it was the sleeve Moran had struck.

Johnny felt like a ghoul as he pulled the gun out from under the dead man. Feeling it all over he decided that it was unbroken and that it was a Winchester exactly like his own. Then he searched the body for ammunition, locating a half dozen loose shells in one pocket. Then he turned away, trying to keep himself from nausea. He had killed other men that night in the valley of the upper Packsaddles but he had not seen the bodies. Now he knew that his own injuries had saved him from a nerve-racking experience. It did something to a man to handle his own dead, even when the victim was as brutal a creature as this one.

He had to stop twice on the return trip, steadying himself with an effort at self-control. He couldn't afford to crack up now, he knew.

Squeamishness could be fatal. Better to get the thought out of his mind and to set himself for the next crisis. Someone else would die before this night was out—and he couldn't let the victim be himself or Toomey.

The very weakness in Abe's voice helped to give him control of himself once more. Even now Abe might be dying because he had done his duty; there could be no weakness in this fight against the outlaws.

The two of them exchanged soft words in the darkness and Moran left the captured rifle at Abe's side. "Don't move if you can avoid it but use this gun if you have to. It's loaded and ready. I looked."

"Where yuh goin'?"

"After my horse. I'll try to muffle his hoofs and bring him back here. If we can shove you into the saddle we'll try to slip away before they can close in on us."

"Got any idea where they are now?"

"No. And I'm not keen on sticking around to find out."

He moved away quietly, halting every few steps to listen. The going was not so hard now, but the sense of disquiet was almost as great as when he had been creeping along the ledge. That night bird kept calling, almost as though in reply to the pair of distant coyotes that were yapping at each other.

Moran could see the bulk of the low hill which had screened his view of the little valley and he circled it cautiously, listening for the movements of the horse he had left behind him. For long minutes there was no betraying sound but when it came—a slight jingle of metal against metal—it was almost in front of him—and he felt sure that he had left the black horse farther around the bend of the hills.

He ducked quickly, trying to outline the stranger against the patch of sky which showed above the hills. As he did so a voice demanded, "Who's there?" There was a sort of grim anxiety in the voice but to Moran the astonishing part was its pitch. Nervousness had almost turned it into a squeak.

"Holy Smoke!" he exclaimed in a whisper. "Is that you, Billy?"

"Moran?"

"Sure—but keep it down. We're in a tight."

He saw her then, only a yard or so away. She was leading her horse but he felt certain that she must have been motionless for some time. Otherwise he would have heard the thud of hoofs. Only the jingle of the bridle had given her away.

"Where's Abe?" she whispered.

"Back there. He's hit. I was coming for my horse. Got to get him away before the rustlers close in on us." Then he asked his own question.

"Where are the boys and why are you meddling around here?"

"That's it!" she snapped, almost letting the whisper get away from her. "Call it meddling when you don't even know the facts!"

"It's still no place for you."

"Maybe not. But I'm here. What can I do to help?"

"That's hard to say. Where are the others?"

"They won't arrive in time to be of any help. Let the story go until we have more time. If you're trying to get Abe out let's do something."

"Right. I was planning to get my bronc and muffle his hoofs with pieces of my shirt. Then I thought I could walk Abe out under cover of darkness. Got any better ideas?"

"Not at the moment. Where are the rustlers?"

"We don't know. We had them down there ahead of us until dark. Since then I suspect they've slipped around to rush us from the side. One way or another we've got to move fast."

"Then let's get at it. Use my horse; he's right here."

Moran took her at her word. He stripped off his shirt, ripping it into four pieces that he thought would be large enough to muffle the sound of iron shoes on rock. The pads wouldn't last long but they should serve their purpose.

"That ripping sounds awfully loud," the girl murmured.

"So does your whisper."

She subsided, taking the horse's head while he worked clumsily in the darkness to adjust the pieces of cloth. It seemed to him that the job was taking hours but eventually it came to an end. "Now ease him forward," he told her softly. "Make it as easy as you can. I'll keep your arm to show you the way but it'll be better if you handle the pony. We don't want him to spook."

It seemed to him that they were making a tremendous racket as they moved along and he expected to hear the crash of gunfire any moment. Still nothing happened and presently he was kneeling beside Toomey. "Can you stand it to sit in the saddle, Abe?" he asked.

"I reckon." The man's voice seemed a little stronger and the sound helped Moran's optimism. With a little luck they might get out of this yet.

"Got any water?" Abe husked. "I'm right dry."

"Sorry. How about you, Billy?"

"Who's that?" Toomey demanded.

The girl answered. "Me. Billy. And I don't have a canteen either. I didn't expect to be riding so far away from the creek."

"No matter." Abe's attempt at humor was not very comical. "Likely it'd all leak out at the neck anyhow."

"Hold the bandage tight and let me do the lifting," Moran ordered. "If you don't try to use yourself maybe we won't start it to bleeding again."

Abe grunted agreement and Moran hoisted him up, aware that the girl was doing a smart job of working the horse into the best possible position. He shoved Toomey into the saddle, steadying him there while he whispered, "Keep one hand on the bandage and grab hold of the saddle horn with the other. We're on our way."

"You'll have to show me," Billy whispered. "I'm completely lost."

Johnny shuffled along to her side, handing her the rifle which had been on the ground beside Abe. "Can you use this if necessary?"

"I'll try. What is it?"

"Winchester. Usual thing. It's full."

"I can handle it."

"Then come on."

They had scarcely started to move when Moran halted them with a sharp hiss. Somewhere off beyond the first rise he had heard the unmistakable sound of a bootheel scraping against rock. When it came again he located it more exactly and decided that a man was working around the low hill toward the outer ledge. "On again—but quiet," he breathed. "Maybe we can give him the slip."

Now their progress seemed noisier than ever, each little thump magnifying itself in their ears until Moran thought they must be betraying themselves to any listener within a half mile. Still no alarm was sounded and he knew that they were working around the hill, closing in on the spot where he had left his own horse. Another twenty yards and they might make a break for it.

Then came the sound Moran had been dreading. A voice hailed in sharp but guarded challenge from just beyond the hill. "That you over there, Red?"

Moran replied promptly, trying to fake the intonation he had heard from behind the boulder. "Right. Who's that?"

"Buck. Got the trail yet?"

"Right here."

"Good. Stay on it and shove toward the slope. Look out fer the old man."

"Right." Under his breath he almost hissed at Billy, "Shove forward. This time it's all right to let him hear the move."

"Where are you going?"

"I'll be right behind you. They must be closin' in from two sides and pretty soon he's going to find out that he wasn't talking to Red. Hustle it up."

He stepped aside to let Billy take the pony past him. Then he stood motionless, listening for a sound which might give him a clue to the location and intention of the enemy. Apparently the two Buckalews and Red were supposed to be up here in the hill country. The fourth man might be here also or he might have been so seriously wounded that he had not made the climb out of the pocket. Better to figure on four; it was safer that way.

He gave way slowly, a little worried by the sound of his own horse moving about. Billy's approach had disturbed the animal and he was shying in the darkness. The sound brought a hail that was not so guarded as had been the exchange of words with the surviving Buckalew son. "Somebody movin' back there," the voice snapped. "Look out he don't git away." A light flared suddenly from behind an outcropping. Before Johnny could even guess at its meaning he was completely informed without guessing. A burning bundle of some sort arched through the air to land among the rocks near the spot where he had held forth at dusk. Had he been there now he would certainly have been easy pickings for a sniper behind the rocks.

"He's gone," a voice stormed. "We got to git after him. Where's the old man? Did he git up with the broncs yet?"

In the light of the still burning flare Moran could see a figure stride into view from behind one of the mounds which topped the ledge. It was a long shot in the dark but he didn't think he would get a better one very soon. Drawing as careful a bead as possible, considering the fact that he could only guess at the true position of his

234

sights, he hammered a shot at the outlaw, turning the rifle immediately to take a hasty whack at the fellow who had thrown the flare. Then he retreated headlong toward his companions. In a sense it had been bad strategy to disclose his position with the gunshots but he thought the merits outweighed the risk. Those two slugs would slow the enemy down a bit and make them over-cautious. Meanwhile, he knew that they had no horses on the ledge. The delay might permit an escape.

He explained it that way to Billy as he reached the spot where she was holding both ponies. "We'll make a break," he told her. "You can climb up behind me. You'll be all right while we travel slow—and Abe can't take any fast stuff."

He was climbing into the saddle even as he spoke the words, completely ignoring Toomey's protests about a restrained pace. "Give me your hand," he said to Billy. "I'll haul you up."

"I can make it," she retorted. He felt the tug on his saddle as she grasped its rear edge and then an arm went about his waist. "I'm here," she whispered almost in his ear. "Better shove Abe out ahead. Then we can watch him. He's pretty wobbly."

"Wish I had a drink," Abe muttered. "I'd hold up fust rate if I did."

"Get going," Moran told him shortly. "There's a canteen on my saddle but we want to put some distance back of us before we lose any more time."

The shouting in the rear warned them that there was going to be trouble in very short order. Moran could distinguish at least three voices and he concluded that the elder Buckalew had come up with the horses. In another minute or two the pursuit would commence.

They moved away at an easy pace, not only because they wanted to avoid unnecessary noise but because they didn't know the country. Riding blind in the darkness was no fun at best. "I think there's a good patch of pine back here on the first rise," Johnny said aloud. "I'm guessing that we'd do well to hole up there if we can find it. We might even give 'em the slip and at the worst we'll have a position we can defend."

"You're giving the orders," Billy said shortly.

"That's different," he commented.

She did not reply.

They covered perhaps a quarter of a mile, Moran calling the turns partly from memory and partly by studying the dark contours of the hills around him. At first Abe seemed to be quite able to guide the animal he was riding, but then his grunted reply became little more than a wheeze and Moran had to range beside him to turn the bronc when it wanted to slant off along a low ridge.

"Steady, Abe," he urged. "It won't be much

farther now. That black mass ahead and to the left looks like trees."

"It better be," Billy murmured. "They're coming along behind us now. I can hear them."

Johnny pulled into the lead then, whispering for Billy to reach out and grasp the bridle of the other pony. In that way Toomey could use all his waning strength to keep himself in the saddle.

They cut away from what Moran believed to be the trail he had used in following the rustlers, climbing a gentle slope toward the dark patch which he believed to be the first sizeable belt of pines. For a few minutes they would be exposed to any fire from the rear but he didn't think the pursuers would be close enough to hear or see the move.

Then an unexpected difficulty intruded itself. They came up against a low but almost vertical cliff which seemed to angle across the slope. That was the explanation of the abrupt end to the pine belt, Johnny concluded. The soil on top of this stratum was suited to trees, while below it nothing but mesquite seemed to thrive. "This way," he said confidently. He had no knowledge of the terrain but it was better to keep the others from knowing about his ignorance. Abe was holding up on nerve alone and it wouldn't do to let him lose confidence.

Fortunately his guess was a good one. Within a dozen yards he sensed rather than saw a break in the ledge. "Up we go," he said shortly. "Take it easy, I'll lead Abe's bronc."

He slid sideways, trying to avoid hitting the girl with a spur as he went out of the saddle but the precaution was unnecessary. She was already dropping to the ground and coming forward to take the bridle of the black horse. "Good enough," Johnny approved. "Lead the way but don't get separated from us. We'll go just far enough in to take cover."

The trees swiftly closed about them as Johnny followed the sound of his companion's progress. Twice she grunted a little as she had to fight her way through thick branches but then she called back in a husky whisper. "Seems clear right here. Shall we stop?"

"Good enough. Tie up the bronc and get the canteen from the saddle. I'll lift Abe down."

Toomey was limp when Moran handled him but he revived a little when Billy came to them with the water. "Divide it between you," Johnny told her. "I had a swig late this afternoon."

He took the other horse across to where the black was picketed, getting the feel of their hasty shelter. It seemed to be a small opening among the trees, just about large enough to hide the horses without permitting them to stamp on the wounded man.

"All right, you two?" he asked, returning.

"Fine now," Billy told him.

"Stay here. Better stick by the broncs and be ready to grab their noses if either of them starts to whinny. I'll work out to the edge and stand guard."

"Be careful."

He didn't bother to reply but the tone made him feel pretty good. She had put something into the words which made him feel that she was not merely concerned about herself. He suddenly knew that he liked the idea very much. On every other occasion he had enjoyed wrangling with her. Now he enjoyed the quiet way in which they had begun to work together. At any other time it would have been a nice sort of thing to think about. Now he could only throw it from his mind as he pushed out to the edge of the pines and began to listen for sounds of the enemy.

Chapter Seventeen

JOHNNY had scarcely taken his position at the top of the low cliff when he heard them moving along the trail through the hills. They were arguing violently among themselves and the sound carried clearly on the night air.

"They got away," one voice declared. "Ain't no use huntin' 'em in the dark. We'd be smarter to git the hell outen here. Come daylight this ain't gonna be healthy country fer any of us."

"Don't be a fool," old Buckalew's voice rasped. "Toomey's hit hard and his hoss is dead. Moran's fool enough to stick with Toomey so all we gotta do is run down two men on a tired hoss. Once we git 'em we're in the clear. Ain't nobody gonna prove nothin' on us then."

Another man joined in to agree and Moran thought it was Red, the grim humorist who had been behind that boulder on the slope. For a moment or two he was tempted to believe that his enemies now numbered but three. Then another nasal voice started to talk.

"Pop's right. If we kill Moran we're safe. There ain' no point in . . ."

"You got a grudge to settle," the first speaker cut in. "I ain't."

"Don't try to cut out on us," Red warned ominously. "We're all in this together. Old Buck's still boss and I'm backin' him."

Buckalew's angry tones took on an additional note of authority at that. "We're playin' it whole hawg," he announced. "If'n we don't ketch up with 'em purty soon we'll risk a light and have a look at the sign. They won't git far."

Moran smiled grimly as he listened to them drift on out of hearing. It helped to know that there was going to be a breathing spell, even though the deadly determination of the enemy was now so clear. Darkness was an ally for the moment; it might provide the delay which would enable help to arrive.

Branches swished behind him then and Billy's voice came softly. "I heard them talking," she announced. "I don't need to stand guard over the horses now, do I?"

"No. Relax and let's have your story. When do we expect some help?"

"I'm afraid we can't expect any."

"Why not?"

"Let me tell it from the beginning. When I left you today, I rode hard for the part of the valley where we had seen the men working. It seemed to me that they ought to be in sight when I crossed the little brook but they weren't. I watched the ground and soon began to see the signs of where they'd been working. Then I found something that bothered me. There were a lot of confused marks. I stopped to look it over carefully. Several men had been afoot there and a big bloodstain showed in the scuffed earth and on the grass. As nearly as I could tell there had been some kind of an accident.

"I saw where they'd all headed for home and a tally of the prints showed that all of the broncs were accounted for. So I went after them. I suppose I'd gone about a mile when I saw Ed Underhill coming toward me. I'll tell you frankly that I was scared, but I put on my best act. He looked worried too when he saw me and I decided that I wasn't doing any more acting than he was when we stopped to talk so calmly.

"He told me that Glaspey had slipped and fallen, twisting that lame knee of his. Jones got down to help him and got too close to a steer they had just roped. The animal gored him rather badly before the others could come to his aid. Both men were hurt badly enough so that it was decided to take them back to the ranch."

"But why was Underhill heading in the other direction?"

"That's what I wanted to know. He was obviously squirming at the question but he told me—rather lamely, I thought—that he wasn't needed and had decided to make a quick check of stock before following the others."

"I'll bet he'd begun to smell a rat and was

getting away. Either that or he knew that this was to be a final raid and he was going to join his pards."

"It was the latter," she said calmly. "I found that out. At first I pretended to believe him but when I watched from the top of a rise I saw him riding hard down the valley, making no pretense of checking anything. So I turned around and followed him."

"I reckon I ain't the only one who has dumb spells. Why didn't you go on and get help?"

"Now don't start any of that silly bickering. Maybe I was foolish but I knew that I couldn't overtake the men in time to get them started back. At least one of them would have to go on with the injured hands. It meant that I would be spending a lot of valuable time to get not more than one helper. I decided that it would be better to trail you and let you know the situation before you could get too far into trouble."

"I withdraw the complaint," he said solemnly. "I reckon I'd have done the same thing. What happened then?"

"I heard shots just before I came within sight of Pigpen. When I reached there I was just in time to help Ella McSorley with her husband. He was shot through the upper leg. Underhill was lying dead by the corral."

"Did you get the yarn?"

"Of course. Underhill had demanded that

McSorley go with him to join the gang. Apparently he suspected that I must have seen the rustler trail. At any rate McSorley told him that he was not going to play along with the outlaws any longer—so the pair of them shot it out. It wasn't that simple, I suppose, but that's the important part. McSorley killed Underhill but was pretty badly hurt at the same time."

"Did he tell you anything else about the gang?"

"I didn't give him time. He managed to tell about the fight with Underhill while we were getting him to bed and dressing the wound. Then I got a fresh pony out of his corral and started to follow your trail. Darkness overtook me while I was still quite a distance from where I found you. I simply headed toward the sound of shooting. There wasn't anything else to do by that time."

"Then no one at Lazy J knows about the fix we're in?"

"No. Not unless someone had come back down the valley to get the facts from McSorley."

"Which isn't likely."

"No."

There was a long silence before Billy asked anxiously, "Did I do it all wrong?"

"You're a stout fella," Moran told her. "We'll get out of this yet. . . . If we don't . . . I'd better tell you now that I take back all I said about spoiled brats."

"Thanks. And you're not so stupid. You had sense enough to fill your canteen and . . ."

"And what?"

"And you were way ahead of me that day when I tried to be so superior. Father made it clear that you had gotten a good line on the whole dirty deal before I returned from Dragoon Bend with my facts."

"Then you didn't pass them on as mine?" he asked.

"Partly I did. By that time I'd decided that my plan to blackmail you over your past reputation wasn't such a good idea. I tried to let my father think that both of us had been learning things— but he was his usual self, letting me know that you'd understood the whole situation before I learned a thing."

He could sense the bitterness in her voice and it bothered him. That was the whole trouble with Billy Whitaker, he thought; she was continually troubled by her father's unfairness to her. "Don't blame him for being that way," he said soothingly. "I've got it all sized up that your old man has been henpecked for so long—and in such a smart fashion—by your mother that he has gotten so he don't want a woman to have a bit of sense. It keeps reminding him of how much he lets himself get bossed."

"But he needs it," she protested.

"Sure. Maybe that's why he hates it so much.

He don't like to admit that his own laziness requires someone else to look after matters for him. A good-sized chunk of human cussedness crops out in your pop. You might as well figure on it and play the game accordin' to the way you find things."

She was silent for some minutes. Then she said quietly, "You're quite a philosopher, Johnny Moran. I didn't give you credit for doing that kind of thinking."

"You didn't give me credit for *any* thinking," he corrected. Then he chuckled softly and added, "Not that I did too much. I've been mighty dumb, all right."

She did not comment and presently he added, "I was awful stupid to figure that you was a spoiled brat."

"Careful," she warned. "We'll be decent to each other if we're not careful. Then neither one of us would know how to act."

"I reckon I could work up a few ideas," he said.

A distant shout interrupted what might have turned out to be an interesting line of conversation. Moran reached out to lay a hand on her arm as a warning for silence—and found it pleasant to leave the hand there. They listened intently for several minutes but could hear nothing further. Then Johnny muttered, "I reckon they've pulled up to have a confab. That means they might risk a light and take a squint at the trail."

"Will it tell them anything?"

"You ought to know; you're the expert. They'll see that we're not ahead of them—and they'll see that there's someone else here with Abe and me."

"They could figure it to be Underhill."

"No matter. While they're guessing we've got a bit of an edge. What time do you figure it to be?"

"Close to midnight, I suppose."

"We've got five hours then. If they don't locate us by dawn they'll not be fooled any longer. After that it'll be us or them."

Abe's voice came weakly from the pines. "Better reload my six-gun for me, Moran. If they git close I kin take a hand."

Johnny moved back toward him. "I'm giving orders," he announced sternly. "You stay flat until Billy or me tells you different. If they get into the timber behind us you'll have to look out for yourself but don't make a move unless that happens."

To the girl he explained, "I'll work out here to our left. It'll put me closer to the trail we were on and I'll be able to see better what they're doing. If they start to snoop around here I can get a shot before they find out just where we are. No use drawing fire toward Abe."

"I'll cover the break in the ledge," she agreed quietly. "But try to let me know when you're moving. I don't want to . . ."

"I wouldn't like it either," he agreed dryly.

"But don't be in any big hurry to open up with the rifle. We'll be better off to delay, so keep the ponies quiet."

He moved away then, feeling his passage through the pines until he was at the top of the little cliff. Then he listened for several minutes before continuing along to the left. Judging by the distant sounds the rustlers were coming back but were still some distance away.

Presently he found a spot where the trees broke away from the ledge. It was hard to be certain in the darkness, but he believed that the position would enable him to see in two directions when daylight came. So he settled himself under a tree, hunkered down as comfortably as possible.

A quarter of an hour passed without any sound from the enemy, but then he realized that a light had glared briefly somewhere around on his extreme left. That would be the general direction of the trail through the hills so he figured that the outlaws were working their way back, lighting an occasional match to check the trail. He hoped they would stop somewhere within range for another inspection; he might be able to cut down the odds without waiting for daylight.

Within five minutes he heard the approaching hoofbeats and the mutter of angry voices. Even an occasional word drifted to him and he knew that the elder Buckalew was still driving them on, evidently having some trouble with a man who wanted to get away. Then they stopped and another light sprang into being. Moran could see only its beams so he realized that the rustlers were still in one of the hollows between hills.

There were a couple of disgusted curses and they started to move once more. "Can't be too far now," a man growled. "We're damn near back to the hole."

The sounds moved along until Johnny knew that they were almost at the spot where he had elected to leave the trail. There Buckalew called another halt. "Light up, Squint," he growled.

A match flared, outlining two riders. Johnny covered one with his rifle but held his fire until the man called Squint set fire to a bundle of what looked like old paper. Then he squeezed the trigger.

The slap of the rifle seemed to touch off a most remarkable set of echoes. Men yelled, a horse began to thresh about among the pines, the distant coyotes yapped a little more frantically, and one of the rustlers started to drive slugs in the general direction of the trees. Moran heard it all without being quite conscious of it. He turned his aim on one of the plunging figures and fired again.

"Missed, doggone it!" he grunted. "I thought I might get two if I waited till the paper was burnin'."

The glare of the flaming bundle still lighted the mesquite but he could not see any of the rustlers.

Every one of them had dropped out of sight behind the rise of ground which flanked the trail and Johnny could only hope that one had dropped with a slug in him. He studied the flickering shadows over his rifle sights, watching the far edges of the lighted area. Any attack would come from the side, he knew; the rustlers would keep down until they were away from that burning bundle.

Presently a shadow moved and he blasted away, sighting as carefully as possible. Again he could not tell whether or not he had scored a hit but he was satisfied to make it hot for them. Maybe that nervous one would sneak away, thus cutting the odds a bit.

There was no answering fire this time but he could hear a mutter of sound which hinted that Buckalew was giving orders. Moran thought he knew what those orders would be. The rustlers would try to slip around so as to attack the woodland from the sides.

"Get your gun, Billy," he called back, keeping his voice as low as possible without muffling it completely. "You'll likely have company. Keep Abe down."

Her reply was an eager, "Did you hit any of 'em?"

"Can't tell. Maybe one."

That was the last word spoken for three solid hours. To Moran it seemed like as many years.

Twice he heard sounds of movement but neither time could he locate the noise. The outlaws were being very cautious, preparing for their big assault with sufficient care to indicate that they had learned to fear their prey. The silence in the trees had been complete. Toomey and the girl must have been even more on tenterhooks than Johnny was but neither of them uttered a sound. Good stuff in both of them, Johnny told himself.

Finally the quiet was shattered in dramatic and surprising fashion. From only a short distance in front of Moran's position there came the frantic scuffle of feet. Then a man yelled, "Don't shoot, Moran! I'm tryin' to help yuh."

Johnny thought it was the rustler who had argued for retreat but he could not be certain. In the darkness he could not even be sure what was happening out there. He could see nothing at all; there was only the sound of a struggle.

It occurred to him that this might be an attempt to divert his attention from one of the flanks and he was already starting to swing around when a gunshot boomed. Because he was turning his head Johnny did not see the flash of it. When he looked back the night was as dark as ever but a man was cursing. Old Buckalew's voice rasped, "Try tricks on me, will yuh, yuh stinkin' polecat!"

There was another brief scramble and the thud of a blow. Then a match flickered into life and

Johnny could see what appeared to be a singularly contorted shadow. Two men were lying there on the ground. It was the second one who was lighting the match, even now touching it to another of those makeshift flares.

In that instant Johnny knew what was coming. Without conscious thought he even knew how it had all come about. The attackers wanted light for their attack and they had picked their weak member as the goat for the chore. The old man must have been driving him forward to throw the fire when the desperate outlaw tried to turn the tables. Buckalew had killed him and was trying to carry out the task for which his victim had been slated.

The swift surge of intuition didn't keep Moran from leveling the rifle. He couldn't tell where Buckalew's shadow began and the dead man's ended but he knew that the old thief would have to raise himself a little to throw. So he drew fine at the top of the dark blur, waiting for the paper to flare. Then he caught the beginning of a movement and pulled the trigger.

There was a moaning curse and the paper fell back, burning fiercely behind a dark bulk which moved twice and then was still. Johnny grunted and swung the rifle hard to the left, fully expecting an attack from that side now that he had disclosed his own position by firing. It was the wrong move. A gun banged directly behind him but at some little distance, its bullet clipping a branch overhead.

He whirled to face the new attack and was just in time to see a jet of flame from the trees. Billy was taking a shot at the flanker on the right. "Doggone!" Moran grunted, snuggling the Winchester tight for another shot. "Now she'll draw fire from him."

The rustler's shot was a little delayed, as though he had been surprised at having his defiance come from such a quarter. Then he slammed a slug into the woodland toward the girl's position—and was quickly answered by two shots, one from each of the defenders.

Johnny could hear the man grunt, so he tried to place another slug at the same spot. Billy took the hint and fired twice more, neither of them drawing any reply from the outlaw. Then Moran swung back to study the approaches on his left. With a man unaccounted for he didn't dare let himself be diverted for too long a time.

One man! The phrase ran through his mind a second time and he began to realize what it meant. In the heat of battle he hadn't quite come to recognize the significance of the swift events. There couldn't be more than one outlaw left. Maybe not even one. The whole nightmare could be over right now!

Chapter Eighteen

MORAN waited a good five minutes without hearing a suspicious sound. Then he scuttled along through the trees, dodging branches in the darkness until he could hear the restless stamp of a pony close beside him. Then he whispered, "Everybody all right here?" He hoped his anxiety didn't show in the tone.

Toomey replied. "Mostly all right. The danged shootin' kinda busted up a good sleep fer me— and Miss Billy's right shaky."

A rustle of movement gave Johnny his clue and he went to her. "Not hurt, are you?" he asked, reaching out to take hold of a shoulder that was really trembling.

"No—but I think I . . . I shot a man." The horror in her voice was something she could not quite control. "I heard him groan when I shot."

Johnny did not remind her that she had fired twice more at the sound of the groan. Probably she hadn't been thinking of scruples then. It was only now that the reaction was hurting her. He elected to try a sort of counter-irritant.

"Who's braggin' now?" he jeered. "I'll bet you

didn't come within two yards of him. It was my slug that stopped the varmint."

"How do you know?"

"I had a good bead—and anyway I don't believe you're that good a shot."

"I can shoot just as straight as you can, Johnny Moran! Don't try to tell me . . ." She broke off with a little laugh. "Never mind. I think I know what you're up to—and thanks. See, I've stopped shaking."

He took her hand, holding it a little longer than was necessary to confirm her claim to steadiness. "I think maybe we're over the hill," he murmured. "There didn't seem to be any attacker on our left so I'm figuring I got one of 'em when they lighted that first flare."

"But what was the shooting directly in front of us?"

"Old Buckalew was holding a gun on one of his lads, using the man as a shield and forcing him toward us to light a flare which evidently was supposed to be thrown into the edge of the trees. He killed his own man when the fellow tried to rebel. . . . Then I got the old rascal before he could throw his torch."

There was an interval of silence before Billy murmured, "Then you think we're in the clear now?"

"I hope so. It's been getting a mite chilly for the past couple of hours and I'd like to have time to grab my blanket roll off the bronc. Wanderin' around all night with no shirt on gets a trifle airish."

Her little chuckle told him that she was herself again. "I'd forgotten about your shirt," she confessed. "Go ahead; I'll stand guard."

Before he could move, however, there was the sound of a groan from their right. Instantly Moran went down, shoving forward to the edge of the trees. Then the groan was repeated and he called out sternly, "Crawl this way and don't try any tricks."

Somewhat to his surprise he got a reply. A voice came in a sort of whine. "Don't shoot. I give up—but I can't crawl. I'm hit hard."

Moran discarded the rifle and drew his six-gun. "Maybe this is a trick and maybe it isn't," he whispered to the girl. "I'll find out. Stay here."

"I'm coming with you," she retorted. "You stay close to the cliff after we go down the break. I'll work out to the left a little. Then we'll have him from two directions if he's trying any sort of trick."

"No."

"Yes. I've held up my share so far and I'm not quitting now."

"Spoiled brat!"

" 'Stupe'!"

He chuckled dryly. "Have it your own way. You will anyhow."

They advanced with due caution upon the dark bulk of a prone man. It quickly became apparent that he was not up to any trickery. He was not critically wounded but he was in pain and thoroughly scared. Moran poked gently at the shoulder wound, putting another of those shirttail compresses into place. This time the rustler's own shirt had to be used.

"You'll live, pard," he said when it was over. "Although I don't know how long. It'll depend on how much they've got against you."

By that time a slight graying of the east was making it possible for the three of them to see each other more clearly. Billy was sitting back and saying nothing while Moran worked over the wounded outlaw but she had been pretty careful about picking up the man's weapons. It was clear that she didn't propose to lose the prisoner through carelessness.

"I ain't worried," the fellow declared. "I ain't been riding with this gang very long. I musta been loco when I tied in with 'em so I'll be glad to git loose with a stretch in the calaboose."

"Were you with them on the horse stealing job over in the Raton Basin?" Johnny inquired suddenly.

"Nope."

"It was the same gang, wasn't it?"

"Sure. But I was over here. They hadn't made up their minds to trust me on a job yet."

"Maybe we might make a deal with you," Moran said quietly. "You're the jigger they called Squint, ain't you?"

"Yep."

"You're a lucky polecat, Squint. When you lighted that flare along the trail I had you square in my sights. Then I decided to take the other man first, figuring that I'd get you with a second shot before you could drop the light."

"It was close," the outlaw told him. "I fair tossed myself offa that bronc when young Buck got it. Yer slug whizzed right past me as I went down."

"I'm satisfied. How would you trade a getaway for the whole story of the outfit you've been ridin' with?"

"Suits me. There's none of 'em left anyhow except . . ."

"Except McSorley and Underhill. Is that what you were going to say?"

"Yuh know about 'em, do yuh?"

"Sure."

"Then I'll talk. I joined the outfit because I knew a jasper named Kent who was already in it. They used the Buckalew place partly as a blind but kept a lot o' stock here in the hole."

"You mean the dip beyond the next ledge?"

"Sure. There's a couple o' shacks there. Most of us hung out there when we didn't have any job on hand. Sometimes we handled stock from 'way up along the upper Rio Grande but mostly it was blooded stuff from over around Sawmill Springs. The idea was to steal only critters that'd show a big profit. The part about rustling local beef was Buck's idea. Some o' the others didn't like it because they was afraid it would draw attention to the hideout here. There was another camp up in the Packsaddles but I reckon yuh know about that. I never seen it."

"How many men in the gang?"

"I dunno fer sure. I'd figger an even dozen if yuh count McSorley and Underhill. Not that the old man was much of a hand. I got it that old Buck had somethin' on him and kinda persuaded him to keep his mouth shut while the boys shoved some hosses past his place. Then they had him. He couldn't talk after that because he'd have to explain hisself on the hoss deal."

"Then he didn't take any real part in the raids?"

"I reckon not. There ain't been no decent raids since I happened along. The fust one was the business where yuh trailed the boys to the hideout in the Packsaddles. There was eight men on the job and only the two Buckalew boys and Red Farrell got back." Grudging admiration showed in his voice as he added, "Yuh shore musta been hell with yer guns that day!"

"Four killed and the wounded prisoner died before he could talk," Moran summed up. "What about the others?"

Strengthening daylight was beginning to show the pain-racked features of the prisoner. He was staring wonderingly at Billy Whitaker but he answered the question without delay. "Yuh got one o' them Buckalew varmints this afternoon and the other one when I lighted them papers over along the trail. That left me and Red and the old man. It was the old man kept proddin' us on. He sent me around here and told me I was to work in till I saw a light. I dunno what happened to him."

Moran explained tersely and Squint grimaced a little. "Sounds like him. All them Buckalews was crazy killers. The old man was worse after the boy got it. He dang nigh killed me before I shoved off over here. Anyway I reckon he didn't have much time fer Red. They rubbed each other the wrong way. It was Red what handled the runnin' iron and he was kinda proud of his skill. Wouldn't take much from the old man."

"Sounds like the way of it," Moran agreed. "Can you ride?"

"I reckon so. How much of a hole have I got in me?"

"It ain't too bad—now that the big shock is over. No bones busted, I guess."

"Then I'll make out somehow."

"Right. I can promise you a full day. Use it any way you like, either to start haulin' outa here or to rest up a mite. One way or another you're on your own."

The sun had crept above the eastern hills when a somewhat dazed Abe Toomey led the way back through the hills toward Antelope Valley. The rest had given him some of his strength back but he was still keeping his saddle with some effort. Moran watched him critically for several hundred yards, then concluded that he was going to be all right.

"We'll likely make McSorley's before anybody else gets there," he told Billy. "I don't reckon anybody started huntin' for us till this morning."

She had been almost completely silent during the period when Moran was rounding up a rustler horse for Abe, searching the dead outlaws, and helping Squint to get on his way. Now she asked curiously, "Why did you let that man go? He didn't tell us a thing that McSorley couldn't have told."

Johnny grinned a little self-consciously. "Sometimes I get sentimental, I reckon. I kinda felt sorry for McSorley. He was trapped into this thing and I got to thinking that if we didn't have any witnesses left from the gang there wouldn't be anything to tie him up to 'em. We could let on that the stolen stock went out through the foothills somehow. Mac did a good job in killin' Underhill; maybe we could pay him off by keeping quiet.

Your father would be happier if he thought it was that way."

She studied him with a trace of smile showing at the corners of her mouth. "I'm afraid I never did understand you, Johnny Moran. You were smarter than I thought—and you do have some consideration for other folks' feelings. I *never* would have suspected that."

"You haven't been setting any records for politeness yourself," he retorted.

"I suppose not. Perhaps I can atone for my sins by telling you that my father is talking of offering you the foreman's job on Lazy J. He thinks you are just the fellow to spruce the place up."

"With the proper advice, of course?" Johnny asked.

"Naturally I would offer my services."

"Complete with sarcasm?"

"Of course."

"I reckon I'd kinda like that. It was kinda fun— and this business o' chasin' crooks is an awful hard way to make a living."

Abe broke in plaintively, "I'm kind of a old coot but I ain't too blind to see what's goin' on around me. That just ain't no kind of a way fer either of yuh to talk. Ain't yuh got no romantical ideas at all?"

"I reckon we could work up a few," Moran chuckled.

"Then let me know a couple o' minutes ahead

o' time. I can't turn my head very good and I wouldn't want to miss nothin'."

"Then you'd better start turning," Billy said solemnly. "I'm going to count to ten and if he hasn't made a move by that time I'll . . ."

Abe was just too late.

Books are produced in the United States using U.S.-based materials

Books are printed using a revolutionary new process called THINKtech™ that lowers energy usage by 70% and increases overall quality

Books are durable and flexible because of Smyth-sewing

Paper is sourced using environmentally responsible foresting methods and the paper is acid-free

Center Point Large Print
600 Brooks Road / PO Box 1
Thorndike, ME 04986-0001 USA

(207) 568-3717

US & Canada:
1 800 929-9108
www.centerpointlargeprint.com